Other books by Deirdre Hutchins

The Paranormal Investigators League series

PIL #1 Voodoo in Savannah

PIL #2 A Hanging in Tucson

PIL #3 Suicide on Sunset

PIL #4 The Legend of Providence

PIL #5 Darkness in Denver

PIL #6 Spirits in Seattle

PIL Prequel: The Origin Story

The Dark Prophecy trilogy

1: Resurrection of the Vampire

2: Vengeance of the Damned

3: Deliverance from the Prophecy

The Daphne Winters Psychic Investigation Series

DW1 The Body and the Soul

DW2 Finding Maddy

DW3 Dropped Dead

These are all available from the San Joaquin Valley Press.

Visit us at www.sanjoaquinvalleypress.com

The Paranormal Mystery Series

Creepy Doll in Detroit

Paranormal Investigators League Series #7

A Novel
By Deirdre Hutchins

San Joaquin Valley Press
Fresno, California

Copyright © 2024 by Deirdre Hutchins

All rights reserved. No part of this book may be reproduced in any form without written permission from the author or the publisher, except for short excerpts used in a review.

Creepy Doll in Detroit is published by
    San Joaquin Valley Press
    P.O. Box 9485
    Fresno, CA 93792
    www.sanjoaquinvalleypress.com

This is a work of fiction. The characters are not based on any actual persons, living or dead. Any apparent identification with any actual person is purely coincidental.

Cover design by Andria Davis Kaye
The cover is a collage of elements from Shutterstock: Creepy Doll by John Arehart and Old House in Woodbridge Ontario by JohninNorthYork

ISBN 979-8-9905729-1-1

About Deirdre Hutchins:
Deirdre graduated from Pepperdine University and currently lives in Oregon, where she works as a marketing specialist. When she isn't at her day job, she writes fantasy and ghost stories. She has published 14 books so far and is hard at work on another. Watch for it at the San Joaquin Valley Press website.

Contents

Chapter 1 – To New Beginnings	1
Chapter 2 – Friends, Coffee, and Ghosts	20
Chapter 3 – The Bungalow in Detroit	28
Chapter 4 – The Investigation	42
Chapter 5 – What Can't Be Seen	54
Chapter 6 – Something's Here	63
Chapter 7 – If the Pieces Fit	74
Chapter 8 – The Paisleys	82
Chapter 9 – The Holdens	92
Chapter 10 – The Deaths on This Land	105
Chapter 11 – Curses and Death	114
Chapter 12 – The Lynching Legend	127
Chapter 13 – The Third Ghost	135
Chapter 14 – Elizabeth and the Curse	144
Chapter 15 – A Curse, a Doll and a Ghost	153
Chapter 16 – Breaking the Curse	166
Chapter 17 – The Ritual	177
Chapter 18 – The Aftermath	200
Chapter 19 – Salamander's Story	208

Creepy Doll in Detroit

Chapter 1 – To New Beginnings

"Welcome back, you two." The real estate agent waved the keys in front of the newlyweds. "How was Hawaii?"

Jensen stole a glance at his literally blushing bride before reaching for the keys to their new home. "Amazing. As you'd expect."

Mia cuddled into her new husband's arm. "If we didn't have this beautiful new home to move into, we might never have come back."

"Well, it's empty, professionally cleaned and waiting for you." Barbara Mullins, one of the top real estate agents in Detroit, gave an admiring look to her most recent conquest: the brick home on Wendell

Street. "You guys are really going to love living here. So walkable, up-and-coming neighborhood. The neighbor in that house has lived here since the seventies." She pointed at the house to the left of Jensen and Mia's new home. "People just love living around here."

Barbara followed Jensen and Mia to the front porch, stopping just short of climbing the stairs. Jensen turned the key as Mia responded to Barbara. "I've had my eye on this neighborhood since I started working at the agency five years ago. I know we're going to love it here."

With a shove the front door opened, and Jensen smiled as he said, "Whether we love it or not, we spent our whole life savings having a wedding and buying this house. We're going to be here for a while."

"Oh, you will love it. I know you will." Barbara leaned forward to wave good-bye dramatically. She wished them well—she truly did—but mostly she wanted to move on to her next home. This transaction was done and time was money. "Congratulations, Mr.

and Mrs. Reiser! Enjoy!" she said as she bounced away in her business suit and heels, the sound of the clickety-clack of her footsteps fading as she exited.

Mia stepped forward to enter their new home, but Jensen reached out and stopped her by grabbing her arm. "Wait! We have to do this right, Mrs. Reiser." He smiled at her as he swept her off her feet and carried her babydoll style across the threshold into the front room. Without setting her down, he shut the door with his foot.

Mia laughed at the over-the-top display, but she appreciated it all the same.

Looking around the room, she sighed. This was it. This was the life they'd been dreaming about, scheming about, planning for and working toward.

She had married her best friend and they were living in the home that they now owned. Not renters. *Homeowners.* She could hardly believe it was all real.

"I know," Jensen said out loud as if responding to her thoughts. "This is amazing." His words echoed in the empty home. The previous owners had done some upgrades, so there were hardwood floors throughout. The bathrooms were in pretty good condition, but the kitchen might eventually need a full remodel. They didn't care. They would save up for that. An outdated kitchen wouldn't scare them away from this dream.

And Mia meant it when she said she'd had her eye on this neighborhood for a while. The ad agency where she worked was only a few blocks away, and when she and Jensen were living in the apartments, she used to cut down Wendell Street just to daydream. She told herself, "One day."

And 'one day' was finally here.

"Let's just take a look around and make sure everything looks good. We obviously can't sleep here until our stuff gets here," Jensen said, already starting to look around and inspect the built-in bookshelves in the front room. In the center of the room was a hallway that led to the bedrooms, and on the right was the doorway to the kitchen.

"Okay. We can sleep at my mom's house

tonight," Mia stated as she turned on the hallway light. Sunlight was streaming through the front windows, so the living room was bright enough. But the hallway seemed ominous, tucked as it was inside the shadows.

"Which room do you want to use as the office?" Jensen asked, squeezing past his wife and stepping into the now brightly lit hallway. "I was thinking maybe this one." He stopped in front of the first room on the right. "I figured it's close enough to the living room that we can still hear if something is being delivered or whatever."

"Really? I was thinking the room in back, since it has those nice built-ins." Mia pushed past him and walked down the hallway, past the bathroom and into the potential office. A stream of light came in through the single window, but it still felt heavy somehow, so Mia turned on the light. "What do you think?"

She stepped in and gestured around the room.

"I think the previous owners forgot something." Jensen pointed at one of the built-in bookshelves but walked toward it anyway. Mia followed.

"Oh," was all Mia could say. Sitting there, on the shelf, was a doll. It didn't look forgotten, it looked purposeful. It was seated and posed, dead center of the shelves, the arms placed in a folded position across its lap. Her face was porcelain and her dress a frilly red party frock. And it looked old. They didn't make dolls like this anymore. This was an antique, maybe even an heirloom. "How could they forget this?"

"I better call Barbara before she gets too far." Jensen pulled his phone out of his back pocket and called the woman on speed dial. Over the past few months of looking at houses, he had called Barbara so many times he was surprised his phone didn't just dial automatically every time he picked it up.

They stayed standing there by the doll, neither one of them wanting to touch it for some reason. Mia told herself it was because it belonged to someone else, denying the real reason even as it tried to burst free.

This doll gave her the complete creeps.

When Jensen hung up, he had a frown on his face.

"What? Did she say she'd come get it?" Mia asked, sparing a side glance at the creepy, old doll.

"Uh, no. She's going to call the previous owner first. But she said she walked the place just before we got here and there was nothing anywhere. No doll on any shelves."

"Oh. I'm sure she just overlooked it. I mean, it's obviously right here," Mia said with a nervous laugh.

"Of course," Jensen said. He stared at the doll with a quizzical expression. Was it just his imagination that the doll was staring back?

"Well, we might as well take it out to the front porch, right? Just to make it easier for the family to pick it up?" This was Mia's gentle way of saying get-this-thing-out-of-my-house.

"Yeah. Good idea." Jensen looked around for something to use to touch the doll, but the house was completely empty. Their towels and blankets and such wouldn't arrive until tomorrow. Deciding to use his sweater, he pulled it off and stood there in his white T-shirt despite the chill in the room. They hadn't turned the heat on yet.

When he used his sweater to wrap up the doll, Mia said, "Oh, good idea. We wouldn't want to break the porcelain."

Jensen didn't reply.

He was happy to let her think that that was the reason, and not that he was afraid to touch this doll. He had an irrational worry that the creepy mojo might curse him somehow. Of course, he knew the worry was completely ridiculous, but it invaded his thoughts anyway.

Holding it out away from his chest and wrapped in his sweater, he carried the antique doll out to the front of the house, Mia following closely. She opened the front door for him, and they stepped out into the crisp air. He laid it gently on the front porch and wrapped it lightly in the sweater.

He stood up and continued staring at the bundled doll at his feet. "There. That should do it."

"Yeah. They can pick it up from here," Mia

added, peering around his shoulder. "Let's go inside, finish looking around. Maybe they left more stuff?"

Without waiting for a response, Mia headed back inside and Jensen followed slowly. For some reason he felt mesmerized by this strange doll, and he chastised himself for it, even as he gave in to the feeling.

When they were back inside, they finished walking the house. Everything else was empty and just as they'd expected it to be. They ended their walkthrough in the back room on the right, opposite the room with the built-in bookshelves. This was the room they intended to use as the primary bedroom.

"I guess they just missed that doll," Mia frowned. "Which is strange because it looks pretty old. It's gotta be a family heirloom or something."

"Well, you know how moving is. Think of how chaotic it was for us when we were packing up the apartment." Jensen wrapped his arms around his new wife. "Now, on to more important things. Where do you think we should put our bed? Facing the window?

Or facing the bathroom?"

"Oh, for sure the window." Mia laughed at the ridiculous question, squeezing her husband's arms tighter around her. "And the dresser can go over there. But I think we should mount the TV. I don't want it on the dresser anymore."

"A mounted TV? Any other dreams I can make come true?" Jensen asked with a flirtatious smile, and Mia continued laughing.

The sound of Jensen's phone broke up the furniture planning. "Barbara! You can let them know it's on the front porch. They can just grab it." The smile slowly faded from his face as he listened to the real estate agent. "What? Are you sure?"

Mia raised an eyebrow, begging for answers with the questioning look on her face.

"Uh, yeah. I guess we'll just donate it or something. Thanks for checking." Jensen ended the call and then looked up at his wife. His expression was one that Mia had never seen. It was worry almost to the point of fear. "She said the previous owners didn't leave anything behind or ever own a porcelain doll. I wonder where it came from?"

Mia was nervous because her husband seemed nervous. But she didn't want to dwell on the doll or where it came from. This was *their* new life. And no ancient doll was going to override that. "Who cares? Let's just throw it away and be done with it."

"Yeah, that's a good idea." As if the mere thought of the doll gave him a chill, he rubbed the goosebumps on his bare arms, remembering his sweater was still out on the front porch. "I want my sweater anyway." Leaving the primary bedroom and passing down the hall, and yet again out to their new front porch, Jensen walked purposefully, leading Mia.

But he stopped suddenly as soon as he opened the front door. "I guess someone else decided to help themselves. It's gone." He opened the front door even wider to show his wife.

"Good," Mia muttered and stepped away from the porch.

"Well, I kinda liked that sweater," Jensen

complained half-heartedly. He was happy to sacrifice the sweater in the disposal of the creepy doll. Having grown up in Michigan, he could handle a little chill in the air.

"You'll have all your sweaters hanging in the closet by this time tomorrow," Mia smiled as she spun in circles like a little girl in the open living room.

"What are you doing?" Jensen asked as he closed the front door.

"I'm spinning. I won't be able to do this once we have a couch and a coffee table."

Jensen just shook his head. "Have fun, I guess. But now, back to the original conversation. I'm going to take another look at both the other bedrooms to see which one is office material and which one is guestroom-slash-future-nursery material."

He started down the hall as Mia laughed. "Let me know what you decide!"

"Either way, I want to paint it. I hate all these white walls!" Jensen called over his shoulder. He was thinking something rich and dark would make for a good office color. Maybe a dark brown or a sage green. He was still daydreaming about what paint to buy when he rounded the corner into the back bedroom with the built-in shelves.

And his blood turned cold.

"Mia!" he called. "Did you do this?"

He tried to keep his voice steady. It had to be a prank by his new wife, although he never knew her to be a prankster. No one else had been here with them. And if she was messing with him, he certainly wasn't going to give her the satisfaction of knowing he was scared.

"What? I'm still dancing in the front room!"

"Come on, Mia. I don't think this is funny." There was an edge to his voice Mia had never heard before. It was anger. This had been such an amazing day, she couldn't wrap her head around what could possibly be upsetting him so much.

Dropping her arms to her side, Mia started walking slowly down the hall. "What? What are you talking about?"

"The doll, Mia."

She could hear his words, but they made no sense. The doll they had taken outside and then someone else had taken, but now he was accusing her of doing something? "I don't know what you're talking about."

But when she stepped into the room, she could only scream.

Sitting on the bookshelf, arms posed across its lap, was the porcelain doll in the red dress. And Jensen's sweater was on the floor beneath it.

"This wasn't me," Mia said, shaking her head violently.

"Seriously?" Jensen accused her, but only because he couldn't think of another explanation. It *had* to have been her. But when? They had been together the whole time.

"You can't actually believe that *I* brought that...that thing back into our home? As what? Some kind of sick joke?" The shock from the accusation turned rapidly to indignation. The number one thing she had always loved about Jensen was that he put her first in all things. He supported her, cherished her. Even before they'd said the vows. This was a side of him she wasn't enjoying. She folded her arms across her chest and snapped back, "And how do I know that *you* didn't do this? Some kind of post-honeymoon test or something?"

The realization that it was ridiculous to accuse Mia—and even more ridiculous that this stupid doll was causing a rift—softened Jensen a bit. His heart rate was still up, and he ran his fingers through his short brown hair in order to focus himself.

"If it wasn't you, and it wasn't me, then someone's been in our house. You go check the front door and I'll go check the back," Jensen instructed and began marching down the hall.

Mia grabbed his arm and slowed him down. "We'll go together. I'm nervous now."

Jensen nodded. He was nervous too. What was he going to have to face in order to protect his new wife? He knew Detroit had its rough parts, but they'd been working here and living here for years, never once feeling unsafe. The city reminded him a lot of a mama bear: rough exterior and potentially deadly, but only resorting to violence to protect the ones it loved. Detroit was actually a tightknit community of people who had been through a lot together—and survived.

He'd always respected that. But now? Now he was rethinking if they could actually live in a city so marred with violence. Maybe this neighborhood they'd coveted was not as nice as they'd been led to believe.

They approached the front door and he could see it was locked from a few feet away, but that didn't stop him from testing the door physically and confirming what he already knew to be true.

"Stay close," he whispered to Mia as he walked toward the kitchen of their brick bungalow. The part of the kitchen closest to the front room was where the sink and appliances were. The countertops were a white tile from a bygone era, but it was clean and functional. Nothing seemed amiss.

From where they stood near the refrigerator, they could see the eat-in area of the kitchen and the windowed door that opened to the back deck. It was frosted glass but it also let in a healthy amount of natural light.

Standing here with the heaviness of wondering who exactly had invaded their home and pranked them with this antique doll, however, the light was neither cheerful nor heartwarming.

Because he could also see this door was locked, Jensen marched to the door and shook the handle, just as he'd done the front. "I don't get it. All the doors are locked."

He looked back at his wife, who stood with her arms tight across her waist, as if the terror would come flying out of every pore if she dared release her arms.

"I'm sure it was just some dumb punk neighborhood kid, that's all," Jensen announced in order to calm his wife. He barely believed the words even as they left his mouth. What punk kid could come in and out of a locked house undetected?

But Mia nodded, mostly to calm her husband in return. She didn't actually believe it either.

And then they heard the laughter.

A child's giggle echoed in the front room behind Mia.

With a sigh of relief, Mia looked up at the ceiling. Jensen had been right! Some kid was just messing with them. Before she could muster the energy to turn around, Jensen was storming past his wife to go give that child a piece of his mind. And then he was going to go yell at that kid's parents.

Mia followed as Jensen burst into the front room, but then bumped into his back when he stopped so suddenly.

And like a record that stops with a scratch when the needle is lifted, the laughter went silent the minute they entered the room. Which was weird enough.

But that wasn't what had made Jensen freeze.

There, on the built-in bookshelf sitting next to the fireplace, was the porcelain doll in the frilly red dress.

And a small voice from behind them said, "Don't you want to play with me?" And the giggling began again.

But when Jensen turned to confront the child who was so clearly in their new home, there was no one standing behind Mia.

Mia didn't wait to process any of it. She ran out the front door and never looked back.

The creepy doll be damned. She wanted to be as far away from it as humanly possible.

Chapter 2 – Friends, Coffee, and Ghosts

"How's married life, Paige?" Duncan plopped his huge frame on the orange couch of their favorite coffee shop. It was asking a lot of the couch, honestly, for him to flop such a large body.

"Duncan, I'm happy. Stop asking how it's going as if you don't believe it's going to work out." Paige just shook her head. All these guys were like brothers to her and she had gotten used to the overprotection. But she did still hope that one day they would just move on from the topic of her love life.

Duncan held his large hands up in surrender. "Hey, it was just small talk."

"I think it's lovely that Paige met someone who can put up with the life of a paranormal investigator." Nelson adjusted his black glasses, sitting straight up like a pole was holding up his spine. "This isn't easy. I bet it scares a lot of girls away from some of us."

Nelson gave Duncan the side eye, which Duncan politely ignored. Sure, it wasn't easy to manage a relationship and travel constantly around the country chasing ghosts, but he wasn't going to discuss that openly with Nelson.

"Nelson, I don't think it's the paranormal that scares girls away from you," Duane stated flatly. There was no smirk, no sarcastic twinkle. He was just stating facts.

Paige slapped Duane playfully with the back of her hand. "Stop it, Duane. I've seen quite a few girls interested in Nelson."

"Until he opens his mouth."

"Girls love a smart man," Paige said, defending her co-investigator. The truth was, she loved all of them in their own unique way. They were all different and special, and, in a weird way, it was what made them such a strong team. They complemented one another.

"I think it just takes the right person. Nelson

will find her one day." Duncan grabbed his cold brew and took a sip. "We all will. And I'm glad you already found it with Greg, Paige."

Paige lifted a shoulder as she said, "Thank you, Duncan."

Duane made a scoffing sound, somewhere between a snort and a huff. "Greg had to have the shit scared out of him to even have an inkling of a clue what he was getting himself married into."

"Well, now he knows. And he likes it," Paige responded. "Which brings me to the topic of the day. Being scared shitless by ghosts."

"I wondered if you had a new case for us, Paige," Duncan stated with a smile. It was always nice to come home, but it was also really nice to be investigating the paranormal. He could only rest for so many days before he became restless again.

"I do." Paige leaned in and smiled. "It's in Detroit, Michigan."

"Oh, fascinating. What kind of haunting are we talking about?" Nelson asked.

"I'm not sure that it is a haunting just yet, to be honest." Paige leaned back and dug around in her large bag for her notebook. She spoke as she rifled through pages looking for the case notes for Mia and Jensen Reiser. "It's a newlywed couple in Michigan. They just got back from their honeymoon and went to move into their new home, but there was this weird creepy doll that kept following them around."

Duncan leaned forward. "When you say, 'followed them around'…?"

She knew what he was getting at. "Not like walking on its own or anything. That they saw. Just they'd go to one room and it would be there. Then they'd go to another and it would be there."

"A cursed object, potentially. That would be a new case for us, Duncan," Nelson stated to their leader.

Duane groaned. "Or it's just someone moving a doll around. Why would you instantly think paranormal?"

Paige shook her head. "They didn't. They thought the same thing, that it was a neighborhood kid or something playing a prank. But all the doors were locked. And they heard laughing but didn't see anyone there."

Duane shook his head. "That's not enough."

"I would love to get a camera on that doll," Duncan said as he ran his fingers through his long, chestnut-colored bangs.

"They tried," Paige continued. "They went back the next day and set up a camera. Waited for about an hour and nothing happened. And then they tried, for the second time, to get rid of the doll."

"And?" Duncan prodded.

"Wherever they take it, front porch, the dumpster, it keeps ending up back on a bookshelf in their house."

Duane rolled his eyes. "This feels like people being overdramatic. It's just a doll."

Nelson crossed his legs and adjusted his glasses again. "Many people have a fear of antique dolls. The natural assumption that there is something sinister about them is not unusual. It's called pediophobia."

"Just 'cause it's old doesn't make it haunted," Duane responded, tattooed arms folded across his muscular chest.

"And just 'cause they're overdramatic doesn't mean they're not haunted," Duncan stated. "Both things could be true."

Duane shrugged and then nodded. They had seen the gamut in their time investigating cases as a team. Some people were easily spooked, the mere wind rattling a nearby windchime making them afraid. Others were excited to be haunted and only looked for validation so they could brag to their friends. And all things were real to the person living with the experience, ghost or not.

"So what are they looking for, Paige?" Duncan asked.

"Mostly they want the doll gone. But I do think some answers would be comforting, as well. They seem very down-to-earth." Paige flipped another page in her notebook. "Husband is an architect. Wife works in advertising. Both born and bred in the Midwest. Happy, young couple ready to start their life together."

Duncan clapped his hands together and then rubbed them back and forth. "Then, let's give them some peace of mind, shall we?"

"I've never been to Detroit," Nelson stated. His baby blue polo shirt was pressed and wrinkle-free, matching his perfect posture in its rigidity.

"Me neither," Paige giggled, bouncing where she sat. "What about you, Duane?"

He sneered in response. "Why would I ever have been to Detroit?"

"Then it's settled. We'll have our first case with a creepy doll in Detroit," Duncan announced.

"It could be cursed," Nelson reiterated.

"It could be just a haunting, Nelson," Paige added.

"It could also be possessed," Duncan chimed in.

"And it could just be two clients wasting our time," Duane groaned.

Paige threw an arm around Duane's neck and,

despite his gruff personality, he didn't pull away. She was bubbly and happy; he was moody and constantly scowling. But they loved each other just the same. "Look at it this way, Duane. Even if there's no ghost, you get to experience Detroit in the spring!"

Duane just stared at Paige with his bright blue eyes. And it only made her giggle all the more.

Chapter 3 – The Bungalow in Detroit

"This is the place?" Nelson asked as he parked the P.I.L. van in front of the brick-covered home.

"Yeah. This is the address Paige gave us," Duane confirmed.

"How'd we beat them by so much?" Nelson glanced in the rearview mirror as if Duncan and Paige would pull up in his old car any moment now.

"It's honestly a miracle that they ever make it," Duane said. "That car of Duncan's is a complete hunk of crap."

"It certainly does defy all logic and reason that his car still gets him places all around the country." Nelson stole a glance at Duane. "Why don't you help him fix the engine?"

Duane just stared back in response.

"You fixed up your motorcycle."

"My motorcycle had hope," Duane said. "There's no hope for that tin can on wheels that Duncan cruises around in."

"Maybe we should get another P.I.L. van," Nelson proposed.

"They could also ride in this one with us. They choose not to." Duane went back to staring at the brick bungalow.

Nelson looked behind him and realized Duane was right. Yes, they had monitors and cameras and tripods, but nothing was really that large. They could fit the team and the equipment if they wanted to.

"I'd better call Paige. Make sure they're okay," Nelson stated as he pulled out his cell phone from the glove box. Unlike most people, he had never grown super attached to his phone. It was used for calls and the occasional factoid to research on the fly, but using it for entertainment was a foreign concept to Nelson. So mostly he left it in the glove box.

"They better not talk to us before Paige and Duncan get here," Duane groaned as a young couple pulled up in the driveway and slowly climbed out of their car.

They had the full, thick hair of youth with wrinkle-free, buoyant skin. To Duane, they barely looked old enough to be married. As the young couple spotted their van and made their way over to the investigators, Duane sighed with relief when Nelson announced that Paige and Duncan had just rounded the corner.

Duane hated talking to clients.

Nelson didn't mind it as much, but he knew he wasn't necessarily good with people. He had his place on the team, as did Duane, but making scared clients feel comfortable and confident simply wasn't it. Paige always told Nelson he didn't know how to "read the room," which Nelson thought was preposterous. He was an excellent reader.

Luckily the couple waited for Paige and Duncan to park the car and climb out before starting up the conversation.

Paige bounced over with her hand extended.

"Hi. I'm Paige," she said. "And we're the Paranormal Investigators League."

Jensen looked around to confirm that no neighbors were staring. They hadn't even really moved in yet. They didn't want to be seen as crazy before they'd even met their neighbors. He was very thankful that their van said P.I.L. and not what the letters stood for. He was certain they'd be run off the block if anyone knew they had called a paranormal investigation team.

"Uh, hi. I'm Jensen and this is my wife, Mia," he explained.

"Duncan. Nice to meet you," Duncan said as he came up behind Paige. "Nelson and Duane are in the van." Sensing the couple's discomfort, he added, "Why don't we go talk inside?"

Jensen and Mia nodded in unison, as if this were the best idea. "Yeah, I'd like that," Jensen said.

Nelson and Duane stayed in the car while Paige and Duncan followed the Reisers up the front steps and into their brick bungalow. As Jensen opened the front door, Paige noticed boxes strewn haphazardly and a couch dropped against a wall as if the only goal was to drop everything off and go.

Duncan ducked his head to avoid hitting it on the door jamb and entered the home—not uncommon in any house but ducking was especially common for him in an older home. Paige followed. Mia and Jensen went inside but hovered near the front door. They presented as two people who were ready to run out the front door the moment they were given a reason.

"We know this can be frightening," Paige started to explain to the young couple. "You wouldn't be the first nervous client we've met. Why don't you just tell us everything and show us what you can."

"There's not much to add to what we told you over the phone," Jensen started. "We don't really come back here much, to be honest. Which is really sad because we'd been so excited to move in. I mean, this is our home. We *bought* this place."

"We've been staying at my mother's, if that gives you any indication how scared we are of whatever it is that's happening here," Mia added. "A newlywed couple staying with their parents."

"It's very unnerving to not know what you're dealing with." Duncan steepled his fingers together. "We are here to get you some answers, wherever this case may lead."

"It may sound strange," Jensen said, looking up at the large man filling his front room, "but I actually hope this is a ghost. The thought of some random stranger sneaking into our home is scarier than a ghost needing closure."

Duncan nodded. "I would agree."

"If that's what we're dealing with," Paige smiled.

Mia and Jensen exchanged a glance. "What? What do you mean? Isn't that what ghosts are? Unfinished business and such?"

"Sometimes," Paige nodded.

And Duncan quickly added, "Hauntings and disturbances can be caused by many different things. Unfinished business, curses, ancient burial grounds...."

"Demons and possessions, witchcraft, violent crimes," Paige added.

"Ancient spirits, Voodoo, or ritualistic death," Duncan continued.

At the looks on Mia and Jensen's faces, Paige wrapped up with, "And sometimes it's nothing paranormal at all."

"But ghosts with unfinished business is truly the most common," Duncan explained. "And sometimes the clients learn to live with their ghosts, once they understand their plight."

"Which we will get to the bottom of for you," Paige said with another smile.

Jensen tried to smile, but it didn't meet his eyes. "Yes, we'd at least like some answers."

Duncan nodded. "That's what most people say. Now, can you show me the doll in question?"

Mia shrugged. "We don't always know where she is. Sometimes she's on that shelf—" She pointed near the fireplace. "—and sometimes she's in the back bedroom. And sometimes she's not here at all."

"Huh. Okay." Duncan began to walk down the dark hallway without being invited. "Door on the left or right?"

Mia and Jensen followed but still kept a healthy distance behind Duncan and Paige. Mia answered, "Left."

Duncan turned the handle and walked into the potential office. There were a couple boxes on the floor, but nothing else. Paige bounced in behind him.

"Found her!" Paige called over her shoulder as Duncan walked slowly over to the bookshelf.

From the doorway, Jensen said, "We don't really like to touch it."

Duncan nodded back to the couple. "Good call. The doll could be cursed, and you wouldn't want that energy to invade your lives."

"I think the doll is pretty in a classic way. Has it given off a negative vibe?" Paige asked the couple from across the room.

Mia nodded vehemently as Jensen explained, "Nothing has felt right since the moment we put it outside and then discovered it back on the shelf a few minutes later. I feel like the doll is watching me."

"Let me borrow your pen, Paige," Duncan said. Paige handed it over and he used it to lift a ceramic arm and poke around the red frilly dress without touching anything.

"If it's cursed," Jensen said swallowing hard, "does that mean we're now cursed?"

"Oh, no. Not necessarily," Duncan explained. "We can't know for sure how the curse can play out unless we know what the curse actually is. If it's even cursed at all." Handing the pen back to Paige, he added, "Where did you hear the laughter?"

Mia gestured back toward the front. "In the living room. We had just noticed the doll on the shelf out there, when we had left her in here, and then we heard a child laughing and asking if we wanted to play."

Duncan looked at Paige. To the couple, Paige said, "Oh. I didn't realize you had heard a child's voice."

"Yes. We've heard it a few times. And sometimes the sound of footsteps, like a kid is running around," Jensen added.

"And you're sure it's a child?" Duncan asked.

The couple nodded. "Yes, it sounds like a little girl," Jensen explained.

"Does it sound menacing?" Duncan asked. "Threatening?"

Mia looked at Jensen and frowned before answering, "No. I guess not."

Duncan shrugged. "So maybe the doll just belongs to the little girl."

"Do either of you know if the previous owners complained of any disturbances?" Paige asked.

"Well, if they did they certainly didn't share that information with us, but..." Jensen looked cautiously at his wife.

"Yes?" Paige prodded. She knew from years of investigating that those little nagging thoughts could sometimes be the missing link.

"Well, they didn't live here very long. They

were here about two years, which seems like nothing for a house you own. I mean, we didn't think much of it at the time because anything could make you need to sell." Jensen shrugged.

"We thought maybe they got a new job in another city and had to relocate. Jobs in Detroit can be fickle," Mia added. "We've known quite a few people who had to leave Detroit because the jobs just weren't here for them anymore."

"Which could still be true, but we'd love to be able to talk to them. Ask them if they ever had any experiences," Paige explained.

"We can give you Barbara's number. Our real estate agent," Jensen said.

"So here's how this goes," Duncan announced with a smile. "We'll set up cameras throughout the home. Try to catch evidence of the paranormal, or a non-paranormal explanation for your experiences. We'll share with you whatever we discover and then we can take it from there."

Jensen frowned. "What does that usually

entail? Taking it from there?"

Duncan shrugged. "It all depends on what we find."

"And what if the doll is cursed?" Mia asked, a slight waver to her voice. "How do you undo that?"

Paige waved a hand in front of her face dismissively. "Oh, there are plenty of ways to undo a curse. Just depends on who placed the curse and why."

Duncan bent his large frame forward as if to speak conspiratorially. "It wouldn't be our first. We encounter curses all the time."

"All the time?" Mia asked skeptically.

"You'd be surprised how commonplace curses really are," Duncan nodded.

"Don't go worrying about curses now. Let us do our investigation and get you some answers," Paige explained with a smile.

Jensen motioned around as if to say the whole house was theirs to investigate. "Go ahead. Just don't expect us to hang around. Just seeing that doll again is making the hairs on my neck stand up."

"Oh, no. You guys can go. We can call you in the morning or you can leave your keys and we'll lock up for you," Duncan answered.

Jensen fished in his pocket and dug out the keys. Duncan and Paige started walking back toward the couple in the doorway, knowing they would need to start unloading equipment soon anyway. Jensen tossed Duncan the keys and then led his wife toward the front of the house.

"I'll consider it a win if we can just find out how to get rid of that dumb doll," Mia said.

"We just want to move in and put this whole doll thing behind us," Jensen added.

"That's completely understandable. You want to get back to living your new life," Duncan responded. "You know, Paige here is a newlywed herself."

She rolled her eyes at Duncan but had the decency to smile and be gracious when the young couple offered her their congratulations.

As Jensen opened his front door, he glanced at the van and then turned back to Duncan. "What's with those two?"

"Duane and Nelson? They're just anti-social," Duncan said with a laugh.

"Ghosts tend to like them more than people do," Paige added with a large smile herself.

Still laughing, Duncan said, "They're honestly harmless. Really."

Jensen responded with a shrug. "We don't really have anything to steal anyway."

And that made Duncan and Paige laugh all the more.

Chapter 4 – The Investigation

"Did anything happen in the kitchen?" Duane grunted at Duncan, his arms full of equipment and cables.

"No, not that I am aware of," Duncan answered.

Wordlessly, Duane dropped what he was holding onto the countertop, thereby announcing that the kitchen would be his headquarters for watching the footage. Duncan didn't disagree. Duane usually used the kitchen and Duncan didn't see any reason why he shouldn't in this case.

"I assume you want a camera filming every bookshelf?" Paige asked Duncan, a camera in one hand and a tripod in the other.

"Yeah. So one here in the living room facing the fireplace and the two built-ins and then one in the back bedroom," Duncan instructed.

"You want me as a floater?" Nelson asked. His role was often to be the investigator who went room to room with a handheld camera, catching anything he could.

"Yeah. Paige will be stationed in the back room and I'll be here."

"Do you think we should set up a camera outside? In case it *is* a neighbor playing a cruel joke?" Nelson squinted up at his boss through thick black glasses. Nelson was tall himself, but Duncan still hovered over him by a few solid inches.

"Yeah. Good call. I'll set one up out front. I think it's most likely they would've used the front door, given the layout of the house and where the dolls were moved to and from." Nelson nodded as Duncan grabbed a camera and began to set it up outside.

"The doll's gone again," Paige announced from the front door.

"Oh, yeah?" Duncan raised an eyebrow.

"Yeah. She was in the back bedroom. I thought she had been there this whole time. Just now, though, setting up the tripod in the back room... She's gone."

With a final glance at the angle the front porch camera was able to film, Duncan followed Paige back inside.

"Did anyone see anybody come through here at any point? Someone who wasn't one of us?" Duncan asked with a raised voice loud enough for Duane to hear.

A chorus of noes and a vehement shake of Paige's head were the answer to the question.

"Interesting." Duncan ran his hands through his long bangs as he mulled over what it could mean to have a doll that appeared and disappeared on its own. "Have you ever heard of a doll that can vanish on its own, Nelson? An inanimate object?"

Nelson flattened his lips as he thought about the options. "Well, there's the possibility that the doll itself is a specter. It's rare but it can happen."

"And be that tangible?" Duncan was skeptical, but open to the options until they knew otherwise.

Nelson nodded. "Oh, sure. Same as people see

ghosts that they think are live people. Until they vanish into thin air."

Duncan shrugged. It was possible.

Nelson continued. "There's also the option that the doll is possessed. An inhuman spirit can make the doll do anything it wants. So hiding somewhere doesn't seem that unlikely."

"Okay. Sounds like there's another option?"

"General occult." Nelson held his hands up like the options were actually abundant. "Someone could have cursed it to appear and reappear. There could be witchcraft involved, tying an actual dead human soul to the doll. Perhaps a ritualistic incantation, whereby someone says the right words and the doll disappears. It's hard to know." Nelson swept the front room with his camera and then turned back to Duncan. "Or someone snuck in here when we didn't see."

Duncan looked at Paige. She rolled her eyes and leaned on one hip, her arms folded across her chest. "And do *you* think that's what happened?"

"Unless someone snuck in the back window, I

don't see how someone could have walked past us all, coming and going as we were." At Nelson's words, Duncan and Paige headed down the hall to check the back room and confirm the windows were shut.

Unsurprisingly, the windows were shut.

"What if this was the little girl's room? And sometimes she just takes her doll back to play with it?" Paige asked. It was the simplest explanation.

Duncan turned back to Paige and said, "Turn on your voice recorder. And ask her yourself. I'm going to go check the perimeter of the house and see if I see any footprints or anything that would suggest someone's been sneaking in and out of windows."

As Duncan walked through the living room to head out the front door, he heard Duane call out, "Can we go dark now?"

"Oh, yes. Of course." Then announcing to the whole team, Duncan stated in a booming voice, "Go dark!" Then he marched out the front door.

The sun hung low in the sky, casting an orange glow across the Reisers' front lawn. It wasn't the deep darkness of the middle of the night, but it was dark enough that Duncan had to use the light from his phone to ensure he didn't miss any nooks or crannies.

For a split second, Duncan worried about what he might find.

What kind of person would be sneaking into someone's house just to move a doll around, if this were some sick joke? Dark thoughts of a large, nefarious man with a deadly weapon popped into his mind. Detroit did have a reputation, after all.

But then Duncan pushed it out of his mind. If someone wanted to hurt them, they'd just hurt them, right? Would they really play mind games with a doll first? It had to be a kid. It just had to be. And Duncan wasn't afraid of a child, was he?

Moving one foot in front of the other, he walked the perimeter of the brick bungalow. It certainly didn't appear sketchy at all. The neighborhood was neat, clean, well-kept. The houses were older, but not rundown in any way. The Reisers' backyard was cleanly manicured with fresh cut lawn and uniformly rounded bushes.

It didn't mean someone couldn't be lurking back here playing a practical joke or planning an attack, but it certainly didn't give off that vibe. This home reminded Duncan of the countless homes he'd been called to in his line of work: a typical, loving family home.

And Duncan didn't see anything.

Granted he didn't carefully inspect each bush or anything, but a quick sweep of his light across the yard displayed nothing but a quiet backyard. As the night got darker and the remaining light of the sun grew dimmer, Duncan felt more and more exposed out here. He did a quick pan along the flowerbeds beneath the windows to see if there were footprints where someone might have come and gone in their quest to scare the Reisers. Nothing.

With a shrug, Duncan turned to head back to the front porch.

Duncan was six and a half feet tall, so it was all the more ridiculous when he jumped a foot in the air when he heard the voice say, "Hey!"

With a heavy sigh to calm his rapidly beating heart, Duncan walked to the fence to talk to the neighbor who had called him over. "Hi, I'm Duncan. You're probably wondering what I'm doing back here..."

"The thought did cross my mind. I know the people in this house are new, but we watch out for each other in this neighborhood. And you don't look like the young man who moved in the other day, so care to tell me what you're doing snooping in his flowerbeds?" The man on the other side of the fence was spunky for the little old man that he was. His arthritic hands were barely able to extend as he pointed a finger in Duncan's direction.

Duncan knew how this must look and he was glad the neighbor wasn't letting it lie. "The Reisers hired me to solve a little mystery for them. Someone's been moving a doll around their house." He decided to table the idea of it being a ghost for now. "You haven't seen anything or anyone suspicious, have you?"

The old man looked up at Duncan from beneath a bushy eyebrow. "You mean besides you?"

Duncan huffed a laugh. "Yeah. Besides me. I can tell you for a fact I haven't been moving a doll around."

"You sure it ain't related to the little girl that died in there?" The old man frowned as he asked such a simple, yet loaded question.

"Uh, no. I'm not sure. Why don't you fill me in with what you know?" Duncan folded his arms as he soaked in this information.

"I've been living here all my life, ya know? This was my parents' house before me. So I was living here when it happened." He paused, looking over at the Reisers' brick home. "Jane Brillow. She was a few years younger than me, so I'd guess she was about seven at the time."

"Natural death? Or..." Duncan let the alternative hang there. He hated to say, or even think about, something horrible happening to a seven-year-old girl.

"Oh. Oh, yeah. It was during the polio outbreak. I was lucky enough to stay healthy but many people weren't. We didn't have the vaccines back in those days," the old man explained.

"So you knew her? Your next-door neighbor, Jane?" Duncan asked. The last sliver of sunlight draped across the fence between the two men, as if highlighting the link between the past and the present.

"Sure, I did. Mostly I picked on her, but I was sad when she got sick. It had been good-natured teasing."

Duncan fought the urge to reach across and touch the man on the other side of the fence. His heart ached for the younger version of this man having to learn about death in such a painful way. "Of course." Duncan rested his forearms on the fence. "Can I ask you a question?"

The old man nodded.

"Did Jane have a favorite doll that you knew of?"

The old man seemed to be lost in thought for a

minute before responding, "I don't know. Seems likely, but it wasn't anything she brought with her outside. I just know that the previous family always complained about laughter and footsteps, and we always figured it was Jane." He craned his neck to look back up at Duncan. "They never said anything about a doll, though."

"That's okay. We can ask them. You've been very helpful, Mr...?" Duncan encouraged the man to fill in the blank. He wanted to know who had been so helpful, but also Duncan really liked meeting people. He enjoyed talking to this man.

"Gray. Elliot Gray." Another arthritic finger flew up into Duncan's face. "And I never caught what you were hired to do exactly?"

Duncan dug around in his pocket, squeezed past gum wrappers and some keys, and pulled out a business card. "Paranormal Investigators."

Elliot took the card, even as he grumbled, "Yeah, you looked like one of those fruity liberals."

Duncan watched the elderly neighbor named

Elliot Gray walk back into the house, as he smiled to himself at being called a liberal. He supposed he had a certain open-mindedness, but Duncan and politics were so far apart on the spectrum as to be comical. He never knew when there was an election coming up and certainly didn't know any candidates.

"Duncan!" He spun around at the sound of Paige's voice. She hung partially out of the window from the back bedroom. "The doll's back."

"I've got something for you, too." Duncan smiled up at Paige. "There may be a ghost here, after all."

"I'll say. I've been in the room the whole time. So unless one of their neighbors is a ninja, something paranormal is going on, for sure."

Chapter 5 – What Can't Be Seen

"I was standing here doing an EVP session. And when I looked back this way, there it was." Paige pointed at the shelf. "And it *is* a creepy doll."

"Is it? It just looks like a doll to me," Duncan responded. Sure, the doll had an antique quality about it, the face was painted porcelain and the dress from an era of frilly lace, but there was no smirk or menacing look that made it seem other-worldly.

"It just stares at you with those vacant eyes. After it pulls a Houdini and disappears then reappears on you." Paige rolled her eyes. "That's creepy."

"Duane will have the event on the cameras as evidence, so we can watch it later. Hopefully, you also caught something on the voice recorder." Duncan indicated the small silver recording device Paige had become so adept at using. Nobody talked to ghosts like

Paige did.

"It definitely will validate what the Reisers have been saying," Paige confirmed. "What did you find out from the neighbor?"

"A little girl died in this house. Her name was Jane Brillow. A polio victim." Duncan frowned at the sadness of it all.

"That lines up," Paige nodded. "I'll still want to do some research to confirm, of course."

"Of course. He didn't seem like a liar, but I suppose you never know that he remembers everything as clearly as he thinks he does," Duncan said.

"So you think a little girl is just playing with her doll?" Paige looked up at Duncan. She was open-minded, but something about the expression on her face displayed skepticism.

Duncan shrugged. "It's possible. That certainly explains the experiences the Reisers have described."

"But you don't believe it?"

"I don't believe anything yet. Do you?"

Paige chewed on her lip and stared at the doll while she mulled over what her intuition was telling her. "We've done a lot of cases together, Duncan. And sometimes we get it really wrong by trusting our gut." She turned back to Duncan. "But sometimes we get it really right. And I don't know. But this doll." Paige shook her head. "Something just doesn't seem right. Something feels...negative."

"Hmmm...." Duncan rested his hands on his head, his chestnut-colored hair spiking out in every direction. "I don't get that vibe. Nothing seems creepy and negative about laughter, footsteps and a magically-appearing doll. Sounds like a kid playing to me."

"Boy, I hope you're right." Paige shoved Duncan's arm. "Now get back to work and investigate. I want to finish my EVP."

"All right. I'll go see what Nelson has experienced." Duncan lumbered out of the back bedroom and down the dark hallway. Houses just weren't made for large people back in the olden days. Duncan felt like he was perpetually hiding in a cave in this house, hunching over to avoid hitting his head on the low ceilings.

When Duncan entered from the hallway, Nelson was filming in the corner of the front room nearest to the kitchen.

From over his shoulder, Nelson asked, "Was there any evidence outside?"

"Of an intruder? No. But the neighbor told me a little girl died in this house from polio."

"Oh?" Nelson turned around, his interest suddenly piqued. "You know, polio was often as debilitating as it was deadly. This little girl might have gotten lucky."

Duncan raised an eyebrow. "How do you mean?"

"If you didn't die, you were often left with deformity or paralysis. It was life-altering. Remember, this was before prosthetic limbs and such. A vivacious little girl could have gone from playing one day to being bedridden for the rest of her life the next."

Duncan shook his head. "Sounds awful."

"Those epidemics were awful." Nelson continued panning his camera. "I could see why she'd feel like she had unfinished business."

"The unfairness of it all?" Duncan assumed.

"Sure. Sometimes we see angry spirits who are stuck here because their life was cut short by another human being, but a little girl whose life is cut short by a ravaging disease can be just as infuriating." Nelson paused and thought about the situation. "For her parents, too."

"Yeah. It's not off the table that Jane is the one haunting this place. Something is definitely going on. The doll just appeared in the back bedroom while Paige was in there doing an EVP. And no one else was in there with her."

"Did you bring the doll out here with you?" Nelson asked.

Duncan tightened his face in a look of confusion. "No. Why do you ask that?"

Nelson gestured at the bookshelf behind Duncan. "Because it's out here now."

Duncan turned around and marched over to the doll. He was so tall he was there in just a few strides. "What the…?"

Sure enough, the porcelain doll was sitting there on the shelf as if someone had taken time to place her gently and pose her with her hands on her lap.

"Paige?" Duncan called down the hall. "Can you confirm if you still see the doll?"

Paige stepped out of the bedroom and shouted down the hallway. "Nope. She's gone again."

"And I take it, you didn't touch her?" Duncan asked.

"Not me!" was the answer that came echoing down the hallway.

"Jane?" Nelson asked. "Jane, did you move the doll?"

Both investigators in the living room paused and waited for the ghost to respond. They heard nothing but hoped that evidence was mounting for Duane.

"We like your doll, Jane. Is this something you liked to play with when you were alive and living in this house?" Duncan asked.

Silence.

"Are you angry you were killed by polio?" Nelson asked, continuing to pan his handheld camera as he asked.

Duncan watched as the doll flew off the shelf and bounced on the ground. "I guess you got a response."

Through the viewfinder of the camera, Nelson saw a crack on the doll's face. "Bummer. I made her break her doll."

Duncan squatted down beside the damaged doll, but still refrained from touching it. "I don't know. I feel like she just wants to communicate."

"Jane? Is there something you want to tell us? You can talk. Sometimes we can hear you on our equipment." Nelson looked around the room, as if he were talking to everyone and no one at the same time.

Duncan held up a hand. "Shh. Listen." They

both froze. "Do you hear singing?"

It was faint, like a gentle whisper on a breeze, but when they were listening carefully, both Nelson and Duncan could hear a soft soprano voice.

Nelson nodded. "I hear her."

"Jane?" Duncan said aloud to the air all around him. "Is that you singing?"

As they waited for the response that perhaps their ears would never hear, a loud thud reverberated behind them, in the corner of the room that was closest to the kitchen. They turned their heads in time to hear the next thud. And then another.

"Footsteps." Nelson stated what he felt was fact.

Thud. The floor of the house shook along with the heavy sound.

"Those don't sound like the footsteps of a little girl," Duncan added.

"The person walking toward us, are you the one who has been moving the doll? Who are you?" Nelson asked.

There was no verbal response, and Nelson expected that if he ever got one, it would be something Duane would share as evidence later. But Nelson was wrong. The response he got was a physical one.

As if two unseen hands had shoved his shoulders, Nelson felt pressure and then he slid across the hard wood floor, past the broken doll and into the empty bookshelf. "I was pushed."

Duncan watched everything with a pensive look. He wasn't alarmed necessarily. They'd been pushed before. But somehow the pieces didn't quite seem to fit. "Maybe Paige was right."

With a small rub to the tenderness in his back, Nelson readjusted his glasses and asked, "About what exactly?"

"Maybe this is all a lot more sinister than just a little girl who died from polio playing with her doll."

Chapter 6 – Something's Here

"It's pretty rare we get this many firsthand experiences at an investigation," Duncan explained to the Reisers. "Usually, we have to wait for the footage."

They were sitting at a coffee shop on Congress Street. From their granite-topped table, they had a lovely view of the bustling activity of the city outside. The shop felt modern and artisan, and for a moment Duncan could imagine hanging out in a place like this on a regular basis.

"So we have a ghost?" Mia asked. The white coffee cup in front of her remained untouched, as if she were afraid the weight of their situation could physically alter her reality and make the coffee just some strange illusion.

Duncan and Nelson exchanged a look.

"We cannot confirm from the evidence we have

collected so far exactly what is haunting your place and why," Nelson explained.

"What in the hell does that mean?" Jensen's face expressed absolute horror.

Duncan lifted a hand to help calm the situation before saying, "What Nelson means is, there are several types of hauntings and we need more information before we can confirm what exactly is going on in your home. But from our personal experiences and from the evidence we collected, we can confirm that *something* paranormal is happening in your home."

"So you can get rid of it?" Jensen asked.

Mia quickly added, "We just want this over with. Whatever it is, just make it go away."

"Paige is at the County Library today researching the property. She'll also follow up with the previous owners," Duncan explained. "But your next-door neighbor, Elliot Gray, informed us that a little girl had died in that house many years ago. And that the previous homeowners also complained of disturbances. Did you know that?"

Mia shivered dramatically as Jensen answered for the couple. "No. We weren't told anything."

"We'll let you know if we are able to confirm what your neighbor told us. Would you like to see some of the clips?" Duncan asked, angling the laptop toward the couple.

Mia looked at her husband before nodding hesitantly. She wanted the confirmation that something was really going on, but she was also afraid that seeing it would make it more real and, in some ways, she preferred to believe she had just had a momentary psychotic break.

Living in a haunted house just wasn't on the vision board.

Duncan pressed play and the footage was of an empty shelf in the back bedroom and would-be office. Offscreen you could hear Paige asking open-ended questions like, "Who are you?" and "Why are you here?" And then suddenly, as if there was a camera trick performed, the doll just appeared on the shelf. It wasn't placed there. It didn't float there. It just materialized.

Mia gasped and covered her mouth. Jensen just kept staring at the screen in what Duncan and Nelson could only assume was total shock.

Duncan pressed pause. "Paige called me in when she noticed the doll had suddenly appeared on the shelf. And I suppose the good thing is at least we know now someone wasn't breaking into your home and doing it." Duncan tried to smile at the prospect of a ghost moving a doll around instead of a burglar. It didn't seem to be doing much to calm the Reisers, so he moved on. "Here's another audio clip we caught."

A few clicks of the computer and a recording of a deep voice said, "Shut up. Stop talking."

Mia and Jensen just stared when Duncan paused the clip.

"Who was that talking?" Jensen asked.

Duncan shook his head, but Nelson answered, "We don't know."

"It wasn't one of you?" Jensen looked slightly

more alarmed.

But Mia actually pushed her chair back as she said, "That's definitely not a little girl. You said it was a little girl who died. That's a man's voice!"

"No, we were told a little girl died in your house," Nelson explained. "But we don't know yet exactly what type of haunting we are dealing with."

Mia crossed her arms and tears welled in her eyes. "I'm not living in that house with that...that thing in there. That was evil."

Duncan smiled again, trying to calm the situation. "You can't tell from this that the spirit is evil. Ghosts tell us to shut up and push us all the time."

"Push you?!" Jensen's shock was growing more obvious.

"I heard footsteps so I asked who it was walking toward me. It answered with a shove," Nelson said matter-of-factly.

Before the Reisers could react, Duncan added, "We can't get rid of it until we know what's going on. But now that we know that that is what you want, we will figure out what is happening and work toward that end."

Mia's mouth fell open right before she asked, "Some people actually *live* with their ghosts?"

Duncan and Nelson both nodded. Duncan said, "It's rare. But yes. Sometimes when the spirit is harmless, people grow comfortable with it. For example, if you had found out it was just a little girl who died of polio playing with her doll, you wouldn't be worried or threatened per se."

"There are such things as residual hauntings, where a spirit of the past relives a moment in time over and over. They aren't even aware you're there. There's no threat and you just get used to something happening at the same time every day, not so hard to live with." Nelson shrugged.

"But that voice in the audio clip. It was not a harmless little girl," Mia pleaded.

"And it pushed you. We can't take the risk. We want to have kids one day," Jensen said, shaking his head.

"I understand." Duncan smiled. And he did. "Physical altercations with the spirit don't always mean something negative, but it does give us an indication that there is something more than just your run-of-the-mill residual haunting."

"Why would they push you and tell you to shut up if they weren't evil?" Mia asked. Her voice was an octave higher than when they'd started the conversation.

Duncan shrugged. "Sometimes they just want you to leave. Investigators can really push their buttons. Like pouring lighter fluid on a smoking ember. We ask uncomfortable questions and poke around in things you would never do." Duncan held his hands out, palms up. "So they get angry with us. Doesn't mean they're evil. Necessarily."

"So how do you know if it's evil?" Jensen dared to ask.

But Mia jumped in before the investigators could answer. "It doesn't matter. I don't even want to know. Good or evil, I want it gone."

"Understood." Duncan nodded.

Jensen leaned on his elbows with a heavy sigh. "So, what happens next?"

Duncan looked at Nelson before answering. "We're going to do some research and see if we can get a theory that aligns with the evidence. That will give us a path forward on undoing whatever was done in the first place."

"There's a lot more evidence. Do you guys want to see the rest?" Nelson asked hopefully.

Jensen shook his head as Mia answered vehemently, "Absolutely not."

Nelson was a bit hurt but Duncan only laughed.

"Let me ask you this." Jensen tapped the tabletop with his pointer finger. "What do you guys think is happening? Any theories?"

Duncan didn't like to presume too early in an investigation and he took a moment to sigh. In that moment, Nelson started rattling off theories. "Most likely a cursed object. But there could be a cursed soul. Or unfinished business with a soul. I'm just not sure why it would be tied so closely to a doll..."

At the look of horror on Mia's face, Duncan cut Nelson off from going any further. "The point is, it's too early to tell. We'll get back to you when we have more definitive answers."

Mia, still standing, tugged on her husband's arm. "Come on, Jensen. Let's go." To Duncan she said, "I don't need any answers. I just need to know when it's gone." She turned on her heel and booked straight out of the coffee shop.

"It's a bit of a curveball, ya know." Jensen stood but moved more slowly than his wife. "We're still in the honeymoon phase. We just bought a house and we're starting this new life together. And then we find out our first home together is haunted. It's a lot to process."

Duncan nodded. "It is. But no need to worry, Jensen. We see this kind of thing all the time."

"We've seen way worse," Nelson added.

"Yes. We've seen way worse. And we'll do whatever we can to make your home livable and happy. This will all soon be a fun story to tell at dinner parties." Duncan smiled and this time it lit up his face.

With tight lips, Jensen nodded at the large-framed investigator and then followed his wife out of the coffee shop.

Nelson let out the large breath of air he'd been holding in. "I hope this is a cursed object. We can't get rid of every ghost known to man. And I don't think there is room for a ghost in that marriage."

Duncan laced his fingers together through his long bangs, holding them up on the top of his head. "Something tells me this isn't a simple curse we can undo with a ceremony. If it was just the doll, maybe. But we heard a child's laughter and a man's voice *and* we have a doll that moves around on its own."

"And it's physically strong, whatever it is," Nelson added.

Duncan stood up and the coffee shop instantly felt smaller with his large body filling up the room. "I guess we compare notes when Paige gets done and Duane wakes up. See if we can't figure out what we're dealing with. And how to get rid of it."

Nelson copied his boss and stood up. "That may be the most important part. Judging by Mia's reaction, if we can't get rid of it, I think we're fired."

Chapter 7 – If the Pieces Fit

"Talk to me, Paige. Whatchya got?" Duncan sat across from his team in the hotel lobby.

Duane was awake but hardly seemed so. He slouched down so low he looked like he could be taking a nap. His hoodie was up, covering his bald head with its large Celtic cross tattoo. Sure, it was colder in Detroit this time of year than in California, but Duane sometimes wore his hoodie when it was hot outside.

Nelson sat ramrod straight on the couch next to Duncan. It was upholstered in some sort of plastic-feeling material, the kind where your butt sticks if you're wearing shorts in the summertime. Luckily, it was early spring and Nelson was wearing khaki pants, so no chance of sticking butts.

Paige smiled and bounced in her seat a little at

the prospect of sharing everything she'd learned today. "Did you know that in the late 1800s Detroit was often referred to as the Paris of the West?"

Duncan was about to answer that no, he hadn't heard that, when Duane responded, "Who cares? Why is this important?"

Still smiling, Paige raised an eyebrow at Duane. "Because for your information, *Duane,* Detroit wasn't always as rough around the edges as it is today. It was once a trendy metropolis where early settlers wanted to move."

He was still slouched and, even with his argumentative tone, Duane never moved a muscle. "And? What does this have to do with the creepy doll that moves on its own?"

Paige sighed. "You have no culture, Duane. I can't help you."

Duncan waved her on, encouraging her to ignore Duane. They were like siblings sometimes. "What did you learn about our case, Paige?"

"What I'm saying is, Detroit boomed in the

early 1900s because of the automobile industry. Everyone knows the famous Henry Ford quote that you can have whatever color car you want as long as it's black." Paige opened her notebook and laid it carefully on her lap. "But I am not sure how many people know that this was already a thriving place *before* Ford took off as a major employer for the region."

"Is this just a fun fact, or did you find something that makes you think the Reisers' house was haunted long before polio came through in the 1950s?" Duncan asked. Duane just groaned.

"I find it fascinating, Paige." Nelson adjusted his glasses. "The history of a location can definitely influence the local spiritual activity."

"Yes. Exactly, Nelson." Paige smiled broadly that someone was following her storyline. "Detroit was a key location in the Underground Railroad because it was easy to smuggle slaves across the border into Canada. One of the safehouses for the Underground Railroad in Detroit was owned by an affluent man named Salamander Guillame. His property at the time was right where the Reisers' house now stands."

"Well, that is an interesting connection to local history, Paige. But what does that have to do with the doll?" Duncan asked.

Paige shook her head. "I didn't find anything on the doll, necessarily, but it's possibly timed with the era. That's how they made dolls in those days. But I do think the male voice is Salamander." She paused for dramatic effect and it only served to make Duane groan again in frustration. "He was killed in the Race Riots of 1863 and his property was burned to the ground. Just like a lot of cities at that time, there were racial tensions in Detroit in 1863 and Salamander was highly regarded as being anti-slavery and a major ally to the local African American community. Not everyone agreed with his viewpoints on this matter, though."

"Okay. I see why you think he could be the male voice we heard. What about the little girl?"

Duncan asked.

Paige frowned. "Salamander didn't have any children. I guess she could still be Jane Brillow?"

"Ghosts beget ghosts," Nelson said.

But Duncan just stared at him. "Huh?"

"Well," Nelson shifted in his seat. "You know. The more people die in one place the more we get a vortex of paranormal activity. Perhaps the various deaths over the years led to multiple hauntings and the spiritual activity has just compounded. One ghost is kinda strong. Two ghosts are stronger. Multiple ghosts are very strong. And so on."

Duncan looked at his team members, panning from left to right. "So how many ghosts do we think the Reisers have?"

"At the very least, two," Nelson answered.

Paige nodded, "Salamander and Jane."

"Three," Duane clarified. When all eyes turned to him, he added, "There's the deep voice, the little girl and the lady."

"A lady?" Duncan asked.

"And we still don't even know who's moving the doll around. So possibly more," Duane added.

"When did you see a lady?" Paige asked, rolling back to Duncan's unanswered question.

"Full body apparition. Standing behind you during your EVP session, Paige." Duane turned his head slightly to look at Paige.

"Whoa! Full body! Why didn't you give me those clips this morning?" Duncan asked.

"You didn't ask. You only asked for the doll clip and when Nelson was shoved," Duane answered.

Duncan frowned. "You could've been a bit more proactive with a full body."

But Nelson placed a hand on Duncan's arm. "It wouldn't have mattered. If we had hinted there was a third or fourth ghost to the Reisers, Mia might've passed out." Duncan really couldn't argue.

Paige frowned, looking through her notes. "I didn't find evidence of a lady dying there. I guess I'll have to do more research." She looked up at Duncan. "Could you possibly connect with the Paisleys? I was going to interview them next but looks like I am back to the library."

"The previous owners? Yes. Nelson and I can go." Duncan looked at Nelson, who nodded in confirmation. "I guess we'll see if they know when the doll activity started. And hear what experiences they had."

"There's probably one more thing you guys should hear," Duane added.

The team waited while he queued something up on the laptop and then pressed play. It was hard to make out completely, but it sounded like a female voice whispering.

"I hear it. Can you make out what she said?" Duncan asked.

"I listened to it several times. I think she is saying, 'Time to die'."

Nelson shifted uncomfortably. "That's disconcerting."

"Wanna see the full-body apparition?" Without waiting for the answer, Duane pressed play on a clip that showed a floating lady appear behind and seem to follow Paige. She had long flowing dark hair and a scowl on her face.

"If there's an evil entity there, it's not Salamander. He's nice," Paige said, defending Salamander's ghost.

"I doubt it would be a sweet, little polio victim," Nelson added.

"So we need to know exactly who this lady is, who is moving the doll around, and who exactly it is that thinks it's time for Paige to die." Duncan frowned.

Nelson nodded at Duncan. "And then we have to make it go away before the Reisers fire us."

Chapter 8 – The Paisleys

"Thanks for meeting with me, Mr. and Mrs. Paisley." Duncan extended a hand to the middle-aged couple before sitting on the hotel lobby couch with the plastic finish. "And thank you for making it easy on me and coming here."

"Please, call me Renee. And you're very welcome. We're somewhat upset we didn't think of calling you ourselves." Renee Paisley sat on the edge of the chair across from Duncan. Her brown hair was pulled back into a neat bun and her outfit was professional and well-pressed. She looked very well put-together. "We hated having to move."

Duncan nodded. He had wondered if the disturbances had played a part in them selling the house. "Before we get to you feeling the need to get out of there, why don't you start at the beginning?"

Renee looked at her husband, Alan. He was weary. You could see it on the lines across his face. He looked like he really wanted distance from this whole thing. With tight lips he nodded to his wife, giving her the acknowledgment that he was behind her doing the talking.

"We moved in five years ago. We thought it was the perfect place for us and we were going to live there the rest of our lives." Renee smiled sadly as her husband scoffed at the notion that they could have ever been so naïve. "Our oldest was off to college and our youngest was a junior in high school, so we thought we'd found the perfect place to spend our retirement and empty-nester years."

Duncan placed one foot on his other leg, letting his bent knee bounce as he spoke. "How long before you noticed anything paranormal?"

Another exchange of looks before Renee answered, "I suppose right away, but we dismissed the little things at first."

"Little things like…?"

"We'd notice things move from where we'd thought we'd placed them. There were drafty areas and strange noises, but all things we could explain away." Renee squeezed her husband's hand. The mere memory of the things they'd experienced made her nervous all over again, as if it could harm them just by living in their memory.

"When did things escalate?" Duncan asked.

"We'd been there about a year," Renee answered and Alan followed up with, "Yeah, about a year."

Duncan encouraged them to continue with a simple raise of the eyebrow.

Renee sighed. "That's when we heard the footsteps and the laughing."

Duncan nodded. He'd heard it too.

Renee continued. "Well at that point we couldn't ignore it any longer. Clearly something was happening. We didn't want to say the word 'ghost'…"

"Never did say it till now, actually." Alan shifted uncomfortably in the lobby chair.

"Did you think you had a ghost?" Duncan asked directly. It was clear to him by now that the couple could validate what the Reisers claimed, so that whatever was haunting that house now had already been there even before the Paisleys moved in.

The couple looked at one another with a forlorn look. And then Renee answered, "Yes. We never wanted to admit it, but yes. We knew it had to be a ghost."

"What if I told you a couple of people died on the property?" Duncan asked.

"I guess that wouldn't surprise me," Alan said. "We didn't really look into the why of it all, but we knew it was pretty active."

"Was one of the people who died a little girl?" Renee asked hesitantly. Her brow was wrinkled up as if the very question caused her physical pain.

"Yes, actually." Duncan dropped his propped foot to the ground and leaned in. "A little girl named Jane Brillow died in the '50s from polio. How'd you know?"

Renee leaned back and her skin went very pale. A slight sheen of sweat formed on her upper lip. "I saw her." Her lips tightened and then she added, "More than once."

"We didn't love the noises and the stuff moving around, but we might have been able to live with that," Alan explained. "But seeing ghosts? It was enough to drive us crazy. And we just didn't want to live that way."

"So you put the house up for sale?" Duncan asked, assuming that the apparitions were the reason.

"We did, but..." Alan looked at his wife.

"You tell him," Renee instructed her husband.

This piqued Duncan's interest. Talking to the Paisleys was proving to be interesting, if nothing else.

"Things really escalated when we brought the doll home from the estate sale," Alan said with a heavy sigh.

Duncan sat up very straight, which only served to make him taller and more like a bear. "*You* brought the doll into the house?"

Renee Paisley nodded in confirmation. She was either oblivious to Duncan's surprise at the turn of events or didn't care why he was reacting this way. "A few blocks away a family was having an estate sale. The husband had died from heart problems and then the wife died in an accident not too long after. It was very sad." She looked at her husband.

"Very sad," Alan agreed, but his tone was more of someone who didn't really care *that* much.

"I love antiques and usually we just window shop. I'm not a collector or anything, I just enjoy seeing classic things. So we stopped at the estate sale just to browse, really." She lowered her voice as if the next part were a secret. "But when I saw the doll, I just had to have her."

"Okay." Duncan's mind was racing to put everything together. The paranormal activity had been there but was mundane until Renee bought the doll at the estate sale. A doll she herself said she *had* to have. It seemed connected somehow in a way Duncan couldn't put his finger on. "What happened after you brought the doll home?"

"After that it was like living in a nightmare." Alan frowned at the memory.

"We heard footsteps, screaming, loud crashes at all hours of the day and night," Renee added. "We were on eggshells at all times, not knowing what awful thing would happen next." She leaned in toward Duncan for the next part. "But when we woke up to a shadow of a woman standing over our bed, we knew we'd had enough. I started packing right after. I'm talking, it was three in the morning and I was up and packing boxes. I wasn't staying there another second."

"Did you assume it was related to the doll?" Duncan asked.

"We know it was," Alan nodded.

"It was like a switch was flipped," Renee said. "One day we're living our lives, the next day we bring the doll home we're living in hell."

"Why didn't you get rid of the doll?" Duncan asked what he felt was an obvious question.

"We did. We tried many times." The memory

of all they had endured was making Renee frantic again. Of course, these events hadn't happened too long ago—they had just moved out of the house and sold to the Reisers a few weeks ago. "We threw it away several times. We tried burying it. I even tossed it over the fence once." She shook her head. "It always came back."

"When you say it always came back...?" Duncan prodded.

"It just appeared," Alan answered.

"We'd come home and it was just sitting on a shelf. Or on the couch," Renee added.

"Every time." Alan nodded.

"But the worst was the time we were sleeping and it just appeared in our bed between us." Renee glanced at her husband and they shared the look of two people who had bonded over their trauma. These two had been through a lot.

And it was clear to Duncan that this doll was the key to everything.

"Thank you for sharing your story and bringing

all these emotions up again." Duncan was sincere in his gratitude. They could have easily blown him off, and even now they looked like they wanted to run. "I know this is hard but it really helps me move the case forward."

"No, thank *you*." Renee smiled with sadness lacing her eyes. "It's been so comforting to tell our story to someone who actually believes us. Our friends all think we were being dramatic."

Duncan shook his head. "Not too many people can relate to what you've gone through. But I'll tell you what. The Reisers can." Duncan shifted in his seat and scooted to the edge of the couch. "Would you by any chance know the address or the family name of the estate sale where you bought the doll?"

"Oh, yes, of course. I mean they don't live there anymore, but I can pull up the address. The family was the Holdens. You'd have to talk to their daughter, Shawna." Renee dug her phone out of her purse and pulled up an address on a map.

"I'll see if I can track her down." Duncan stood

after scribbling down the address. "I need to know the history of that doll." *And why Renee felt compelled to buy it.*

The apparition of the lady seemed to be the strongest ghost in the house and she hadn't appeared until the doll did. What was her story? And how was she connected to the doll? And was she the one moving it around, or was she just another ghost and someone else was still pulling the strings?

Duncan suddenly felt like calling Paige.

Chapter 9 – The Holdens

"Her name is Barbara," Jensen told Duncan. They stood on the Reisers' front porch, because Mia and Jensen refused to go inside. "She's the one who sold us the house. If she doesn't know who sold the Holdens' property, she can probably look it up in the system."

He handed the real estate agent's business card to Duncan. It was bright yellow with a photo of a woman who looked like she was trying to be the next top model. It said "top agent" and that felt like good enough credentials to Duncan.

He knew nothing about real estate. His only encounter with buying and selling real estate was when people called him when they were remodeling their new home, or moving in like the Reisers, and suddenly realized their dream home was haunted. He couldn't imagine himself as a homeowner. He wasn't even sure he would be a good one. Just didn't seem to fit with his lifestyle, not to mention the fact he doubted he'd ever be able to afford something in Southern California.

But if he did buy a home, he'd be the one person who *hoped* his house was haunted. He didn't really love living alone. His apartment was really just a place he slept in occasionally. And rarely cleaned.

"I'll call her today," Duncan assured the Reisers.

"So you're getting close to solving this? Making the ghost go away?" Jensen asked hopefully. While she was silent, it was clear to see that Mia felt the same way. Her eyes were pleading to hear the news the ghost would be gone by morning.

Duncan hated to lie, but the words Nelson had spoken earlier about the Resiers not being able to handle the knowledge that there were likely multiple ghosts came echoing inside his head. He decided to stay vague on details until they at least had a path to resolution.

"Definitely getting close to piecing everything together." Duncan smiled. "In fact, we're going to try and talk to whoever's haunting your house right now. See if they'll just come right out and tell us."

Jensen looked at his wife and they both smiled so warmly that Duncan had to choke down his guilt.

"So, if they just tell you who they are, you'll connect it to why they died and then know how to settle their unfinished business. This sounds like a great plan. Thank you, Duncan!" Jensen held out a hand to the large investigator, and Duncan shifted Barbara's business card to his other hand so he could shake it back.

Before their handshake was even done, Mia grabbed Duncan and pulled him into a strong embrace. "Thank you," she whispered. And when she pulled away, tears glistened in her eyes.

"Duncan." The front door opened and Nelson poked his head out. "We got something." And then just as fast as he popped out, Nelson popped back inside.

Duncan turned back to his clients and Jensen

just waved him on. "Go. Go find out who's haunting our home so you can make them go away."

Duncan watched as they bounced down the stairs. They were so elated at the prospect of this haunting being close to done that Duncan had to smile. Although he felt the heavy weight of this burden. It was why he hated to lie. This case was definitely more complicated than a simple haunting and the path to resolution might not be simply burning sage. And Duncan really detested being the destruction of the newlywed couple's happiness.

Nothing left to do but get the job done as efficiently as possible. So Duncan entered the brick bungalow with lowered head so as to avoid cracking his forehead on their low doorframe.

"I've got to call the Holdens. Find out more about where that doll came from," Duncan announced.

"Wait. You need to see this first." Nelson gestured to Duane, who silently walked over to Duncan with the laptop open. He shoved it into Duncan's arms and pressed play for the large investigator.

Duncan watched as the sound of a child's laughter preceded two dark shadows floating across the main room they were currently standing in. One shadow was smaller, most likely the little girl, Jane Brillow.

"This is great footage!" And Duncan meant it. Sounds were much more common, but apparitions were rare and much harder to catch on film. "This just happened?"

"Yes. I want to say it seemed like maybe they were playing tag or something. It didn't seem negative. Until..." Nelson looked at Duane who grunted in response.

"Until?" Duncan looked from Nelson to Duane. Duane might have been a man of few words, but when he did speak it was often with an insightfulness that Duncan completely admired. But Nelson was very knowledgeable with the paranormal and various types of hauntings. So either one was more than welcome to answer his question.

"Until the woman showed up." Nelson

frowned.

"She's pulling the strings around here," Duane added. "And she feels like a woman scorned for sure."

"She's very angry," Nelson agreed.

"What exactly happened?" Duncan handed the laptop back to Duane as he listened to the experience his team had had.

"Well for starters, this." Nelson turned around and showed Duncan the back of his neck. Three large red marks swooped across his neck from ear to shoulder. They were red and puffy, as if they'd just happened.

"She doesn't like us filming," Duane said, rolling his eyes.

"This happened while the Reisers were on the front porch?" Duncan couldn't believe how close his frightened clients were to witnessing such an event. When Nelson nodded, Duncan let out a long, slow whistle.

"Nelson must look like her jilted lover. She's thrown him and scratched him now," Duane added.

"That's amazing," Duncan said, his voice in total awe. "We need to talk to this lady. Find out who she is."

"I'm not asking," Nelson stated wide-eyed. "She hates me."

"I'm sure you've just been in the wrong place at the wrong time," Duncan said, fishing his phone out of his pocket. "Let me just call the Holdens and get the scoop on the doll, and then I can try asking her some questions. Duane, will you set up for a séance?"

Without answering, Duane began fulfilling the request as Duncan dialed Barbara's number.

Without giving away the Holdens number, Barbara dialed them into the call with Duncan as a three-way conversation. Yes, she wanted to protect their privacy, but there may have also been the teeniest-tiniest desire to learn for herself exactly what was going on.

"Hello, this is Shawna." The woman's voice on the line was upbeat and cheerful. He had no idea what this Shawna Holden looked like, but in his mind he saw a relative of Paige. They gave off similar vibes.

"Shawna, thank you for talking to me. I'm Duncan with the Paranormal Investigators League. I'm calling about an older, possibly antique, ceramic doll you sold at an estate sale about a year ago."

Silence. "Oh." The vibe had completely shifted to one of caution. The bubbly personality had popped and left concern and anxiety floating in its wake.

"I'm a paranormal investigator. A ghost hunter, if you will," Duncan felt the need to explain. "So there really isn't much you can tell me that I haven't already heard."

A small sigh escaped the phone and Duncan was surprised to hear it was Barbara and not Shawna who had made it. Judgment, he supposed. She probably assumed he was a witch doctor or something.

But it had the intended effect on Shawna and she began talking. Slowly and methodically, but talking nonetheless. "That creepy old thing was in my parents' house when we moved in. My mom…was partial to it. So we never got rid of it."

"Did your parents ever try to get rid of it, that you know of?" Duncan asked.

"No, I don't believe so. My mom was always... It's hard to explain. Like mesmerized by it or something. I hated it."

"Why did you hate it?"

"It's creepy and...well, I think it's evil."

"Did you ever notice it in any particularly strange circumstances?"

"What do you mean?"

Duncan cleared his throat. "Did it ever move around by itself or things like that?"

Barbara snorted into the phone, as if the idea of this creepy doll moving about was the most ridiculous thing she'd ever heard. She might feel differently if she'd seen it happen.

But Shawna proceeded with answering the question. "Oh, yeah. I mean, I never *saw* it with my own two eyes, but it was always popping up in places where we knew we hadn't left it. Like we'd wake up with it in our beds with us as if it was a teddy bear or something. Ugh."

So that was definitely a similarity to the Paisleys' experience. And likely the Reisers would have woken up to a creepy doll between them had they spent a single night here.

So Duncan asked, "Do you know where your parents found the doll? Do they know anything about the history?"

But whatever answer Shawna gave, Duncan didn't hear it because his phone was knocked from his hand and it went flying to the other side of the room, skidding to a stop against the bookshelf. Duane was in the kitchen by now and Nelson was in the corner near the kitchen. When he caught Duncan's eye, he simply shrugged.

"My guess is the lady ghost," Nelson stated.

Duncan just shook his head as he walked to get his phone. He could hear Shawna through the receiver saying, "Are you still there?"

"I'm here." Duncan bent to pick up the phone and something pushed his behind to send him forward as he was leaning over. He narrowly avoided doing a somersault into the bookshelf by rolling onto his side with a heavy thud. No one wants to see a large man go ass-over-tea-kettle into a bookshelf, whether they're alive or dead.

"Are you okay?" Both Barbara and Shawna seemed truly concerned at the thud they heard.

Finally able to get the phone back to his ear, he answered, "Yeah. Just seems like someone doesn't want me to get too close to the truth." He rubbed the small of his back, which was aching from the fall.

"I don't know where that doll came from, but it was the source of every fight I ever remember having in our home when I was younger. You need to be careful," Shawna cautioned the investigator based on her own negative personal experiences.

"What kind of fights?" Duncan asked.

Shawna let out a puff of air before answering. "We all hated it and wanted it gone. Only my mom liked it and she would argue with us like *we* were the crazy ones."

"And before you moved to that house, this doll was never in your family? Not an heirloom or anything?" Duncan had to ask even though he suspected he knew the answer.

"Oh, God, no. It just appeared in my parents' home and I couldn't wait to get rid of it," Shawna answered.

"Thank you, Shawna. You've been very helpful," Duncan affirmed as he hung up the phone with the previous owner of the doll and the nosy real estate agent. Turning to Nelson, he added, "We need to find out who that lady ghost is who hates you. She's somehow connected with that doll. And get this, both Mrs. Holden and Mrs. Paisley were borderline obsessed with the doll."

"Oh." Nelson wrinkled his brow in thought. "That does sound like a curse."

"But when I started asking more about the origin of the doll, the lady ghost got angry with me and pushed me."

Nelson smiled. "I did notice that. And secretly

I was happy to not be the object of her anger that time."

Duncan raised a brow at Nelson and sarcastically said, "Well, thank you for sharing."

"Séance is ready," Duane announced.

Duncan hopped over to where Duane had set up the circle of tealight candles. "Good. I really want to ask this lady ghost some questions."

And then the front door burst wide open with a swirl of energy.

"I've got it!" Paige announced as she sprung through the front door, a smug smile lighting up her face like the fat cat after its triumphant feast. "I know exactly who the three ghosts are."

Chapter 10 – The Deaths on This Land

"Whatcha got for us, Paige?" Duncan asked, the séance temporarily suspended. They could always follow up with information they'd gleaned from Paige's update.

"Let me show you this." Paige looked around the mostly empty room before setting her sights on one of the larger cardboard moving boxes. She opened her large shoulder bag and pulled out a roll of paper that had been jutting out one side of the bag. She unrolled it and laid it flat on the box. Without explanation, she gestured for the guys to take a look.

Duncan and Nelson approached, but Duane hung back by the séance he'd set up. He knew he'd get the details from the team.

"What are we looking at, Paige?" Duncan asked. He saw surveyor's notes, complete with boundary lines and landmarks.

"This is Salamander Guillame's property in 1860." Paige pointed at the top corner where someone had written in the finest calligraphy, "*S. Guillame, 1860.*" She slid her finger down to point out various sections of the map with her finger. "This is his property line and here is where his house stood." She slid her finger down some more. "And this is where his barn was located." She looked up at Duncan. "And where he hid the escaped slaves he was helping smuggle to freedom on the Underground Railroad."

Duncan stood up and folded his arms across his chest. "I'm with you so far."

Paige dug around in her bag and then pulled out some more printed pages. There was only one photo and it showed a sepia-toned image of a man in a suit with the type of handle-bar mustache that was very typically seen in the Civil War era. "That's Salamander. He was handsome and wealthy. And obviously anti-slavery. Most of the articles I found focused solely on Salamander as this lone-wolf, conquering hero. One man against the establishment kind of thing."

"But?" Duncan asked as Nelson leaned in around Duncan's shoulder to get a better look at Salamander, the freedom fighter.

"But this story paints a different picture." She pointed at the pages Duncan held in his hand. "This story says one of the women he'd helped free along the way decided to stay and help Salamander."

"So, kind of like Harriet Tubman?" Nelson asked. "She wanted to pay it forward and help other slaves have a chance at freedom?"

Paige smiled with conspiratorial glee. "Well. No doubt she definitely wanted to help other slaves have their chance at freedom. But no. In this story, she stayed because she and Salamander were an item." She bounced and squealed. "They were in love."

"I see," Nelson responded. "They were a sort of slave-freeing power couple. I like that."

"Clearly there's more," Duane groaned from the other side of the room. When all eyes turned to him, he added, "Ghost lady is angry. And obsessed with this freaky doll."

"He's right, Paige." Duncan turned back to her with a frown. "Was there anything in the story that might suggest she had unfinished business?"

Paige nodded, still grinning. "It's on page six."

Duncan flipped through some pages half-heartedly. He didn't actually plan on reading the story. He just wanted the highlights from the work Paige had done.

"They couldn't marry. I guess back then it was actually illegal to have an inter-racial marriage. Did you know that? So weird." Paige shook her head. "And of course a rich, white man with a kind heart is a good catch. Eventually, he got married. And not to Esther, the former slave he'd helped set free." She turned the page in Duncan's hand and pointed at an inset photo of a Caucasian couple. "This is Salamander and the woman he married in 1862. Her name is Elizabeth."

"So, Esther stays with Salamander instead of

fleeing to Canada where she'll be free because she loves him? And then he goes and marries another woman?" Duncan asked. And at Paige's nod of affirmation, Duncan let out a long slow whistle. "Yep. That'll do it."

"So, we have a love triangle and it's clear why she's angry," Nelson stated. "What's the tie to the doll?"

Paige frowned. "I'm not sure. Nothing I read mentioned any doll. But at least we know the three ghosts now."

"We do?" Duane asked skeptically.

"Of course. Jane, Salamander and Esther." Paige looked smugly at Duane for doubting her information.

"Did you get any details on their deaths, by chance? I mean, what ties Salamander to the Reisers' house?" Duncan asked.

"Salamander died of old age, but Esther eventually left and went to Canada. After that, I didn't find much about her," Paige answered with a frown.

Duncan exchanged a look with Nelson and then followed it up with his hands in his long bangs. "I don't know then. Why would Salamander be haunting this place if he lived a happy life and died a natural death?"

"Because." Paige put her hands on her hips. "Society forced him to marry Elizabeth but he was never happy. He pined for Esther the rest of his days."

"Do you actually know that? Or is it what you want to believe?" Duncan asked her.

Paige exhaled. "Well, I guess I just inferred. But this is his land. His house was located near this house. See how it lines up? Why would anyone else be haunting Salamander's land?"

"There's definitely a lot here to go on," Nelson agreed. "A jilted lover, the Underground Railroad, possibly violence of some sort on the land. Hauntings have been based on less."

"Thank you, Nelson." Paige nodded at her co-investigator.

"I think the missing piece is still the doll," Duncan said. "Let's assume you're right on who the three ghosts are. How did Esther get tied to the doll? She's clearly connected to it somehow."

From over where he stood across the room, leaning up against the wall, Duane said, "Can we just ask her now?"

"Oh, yeah. We were going to do a séance," Duncan told Paige, as if she needed an explanation for the set-up. Nelson, Duncan and Paige joined Duane on the side of the room closest to the kitchen.

They had just sat down in a circle around the tealights when the disembodied footsteps started.

"There's already some activity," Nelson announced.

Duncan smiled. "Good. Hopefully that will make this an easy process." He couldn't help but think of Mia and Jensen and how badly they wanted this paranormal activity gone from their lives. If they could just get some answers on how to give the three spirits some peace, perhaps they could give the Reisers their lives back. "Let's hold hands."

The team complied. Paige had just started

humming when all the candle lights went out.

"What the hell?" Duane scoffed.

"I guess Esther doesn't want a séance," Nelson stated with a frown.

Duane started relighting all the candles as Duncan asked the air around him, "Esther? Is that you?" A pause and silence. "Are you the one haunting this home?" And taking a giant risk he added, "How are you attached to the doll?"

"Over there!" Paige pointed behind Duncan at a small shadow figure. "I think that's Jane."

Duncan peered over his shoulder. By the stature and the outline, he could assume it was a small child—or at least it appeared that way. There were no distinguishing features. "Jane? Is that you?"

"She won't let me go." The voice coming from the shadow figure was soft like a whisper, but clear in her words.

"Who won't? Esther?" Duncan asked.

"She needs souls."

Duncan looked back at Paige before asking,

"Needs souls for what?"

"The doll."

Paige raised an eyebrow, but before they could ask anymore, the child shadow figure screamed and the tealight candles Duane had just relit scattered all across the floor in every direction.

"Aw, come on," Duane yelled at the angry spirit who had just destroyed his séance for the second time.

And with a final blood-curdling scream echoing all around the investigators, the antique doll fell with a thud right in the middle of the séance circle.

Duncan reached for the doll and Nelson grabbed his arm.

"Don't!" Nelson instructed. "I have no doubt now. This doll is cursed."

Chapter 11 – Curses and Death

"So what do we do now?" Paige asked Nelson and Duncan as Duane silently cleaned up the stunted séance.

"We'll need an expert to tell us what they can about this doll," Duncan frowned.

"There's a local demonologist we can call. I would love to interview him for my book anyway," Nelson said.

"But who would want to curse Esther? She was a good person and sacrificed her own happiness for her true love, Salamander." Paige pouted as she folded her arms across her chest with defiance at the mere notion of good people being cursed.

Duncan shook his head. "We don't know for sure that it's Esther, Paige. And even assuming it is, we don't know what happened to her after she left the

Underground Railroad. Just being an African American woman helping to free slaves is enough to get her cursed by someone."

Still pouting, Paige responded, "Okay. That's fair."

"His name is Albert Dupree. He's a professor at Wayne State University and wrote the premiere book on the intercept between witchcraft and demonology, and how it's affected our modern world." Nelson stood up and dusted off his khakis.

Paige rolled her eyes. "Sounds like a real pick-me-up."

"It's the type of book I dream of writing one day," Nelson responded, ignoring her sarcasm. "Absolutely fascinating. But most importantly, there's one whole chapter on cursed objects."

"Sounds like the perfect person to talk to next." Duncan also stood, filling the small bungalow as he did.

"I'd prefer to keep researching Esther." Paige shook her head. "It just doesn't make sense and I need more information."

"Good idea," Duncan responded before turning to Duane. "Duane, coming with?"

Duane grunted in response and pointed at the location where the child-sized shadow figure had once stood. "Footage."

"All right. Nelson and I will head out to track down Albert Dupree, the demonologist. Can I use a duffle bag to transport the doll?" Duncan asked Duane. "I don't want to touch it."

Wordlessly, Duane tossed an empty duffel bag where equipment had once been held. Duncan didn't catch it. After picking up the bag where it had fallen unceremoniously to the floor, he used the sides of the bag to scoop the doll and let it fall inside. Without knowing what the curse was, touching the doll could be very dangerous.

Over his large shoulder toward Nelson, Duncan stated, "Let's go."

The drive to Wayne State University was smooth and they made it there in ten minutes. Parking was a nightmare, but once they'd found a metered spot on Kirby, they walked toward a sleek gray building with sharp lines and edges.

A man in jeans with a sweater vest met them at the steps. His hair was reddish brown with a dusting of gray at the temples. With a full beard and glasses, he was both esteemed and approachable. He portrayed the kind of laid-back college professor Duncan would have appreciated had he gone to college.

"Albert Dupree." He extended his hand with a warm smile. Nelson and Duncan both took note that he had pronounced his first name 'Albear" and not with the t sound they had been using.

"Duncan and Nelson, Paranormal Investigators League," Duncan introduced as he shook Albert's hand.

Albert pointed at the duffel bag in Duncan's hand. "May I see it?"

Right there on the steps, Duncan unzipped the bag and held it open just enough for Albert to get a good look. His eyes widened at the seemingly innocuous porcelain doll.

"Let's get this into the lab. I'd like to run some

tests." As if they'd brought him some sort of precious gift, Albert Dupree expressed joy at the prospect of a cursed object to study.

"We'll follow you." Duncan gestured at the professor.

The investigators followed Albert inside and down a long hallway.

"It's very common to be afraid of dolls, actually." Professor Dupree unlocked a door and opened it for Duncan and Nelson. "It's called 'pediophobia'."

Nelson nodded. "Yes, the fear of dolls or inanimate objects that look like children. Not to be mistaken with pedophobia, which is the fear of actual children."

Albert nodded. "A learned man, I see."

Duncan responded on Nelson's behalf. "Nelson used his education in electromagnetics to be an amazing paranormal investigator."

Albert smiled. "I respect that. As a professor of demonology, I know how the line between science and faith can blur quite easily."

Nelson smiled back. "It's all one and the same to me."

Duncan knew Nelson always felt more at home in a lab with a professor he respected, and Professor Dupree was no different. Nelson seemed as natural in this environment as Duncan was in a haunted house.

Albert pulled a few bottles off a shelf. "Let's see that doll." He put on rubber gloves and pulled the doll out of the duffel bag. "First, we need to determine that this item is in fact cursed. Then, we'll see what kind of curse we're dealing with."

"And then we can undo it, right?" Duncan asked. He had dealt with curses before and from experience had learned that the key was knowing what to undo.

"Not necessarily. Depends on the curse," Albert said flatly. He laid the doll on the table and then pulled out an EMF detector.

Nelson frowned. "I'm disappointed that I hadn't done that yet." And at the lights dancing across the tool, he added, "Look at those numbers."

"Does this mean the doll is cursed?" Duncan asked, leaning in to see the EMF detector.

"It means the doll is giving off energy," Albert explained. "Which is potentially paranormal. Without an energy source, a porcelain doll should not be giving EMF readings like these."

"There's definitely a haunting associated with this doll. We have video evidence of three ghosts. Could that be related to the EMF readings?" Duncan asked.

Albert shook his head. "No. Ghosts are not tied to objects unless they are cursed. Only demons or inhuman spirits can possess inanimate objects like dolls." He smiled at the investigators. "So next we'll confirm if we are dealing with a demon or not."

Albert lifted one of the bottles he'd gathered and poured the clear liquid on the doll. It rolled off easily, leaving a glistening sheen of moisture. "No reaction. Doesn't seem to be unholy."

"Holy water, I assume?" Duncan asked and

Albert nodded his confirmation.

"So it's not a demon but there's definitely something triggering EMF. How do we confirm a curse?" Nelson asked, truly curious.

"Just like any spell, curses need a reactant. Spells are simply words without the emotion charging the curse and an agent to seal the deal." Albert pulled a lighter and flicked a flame. "Fire is one of the most common reactants."

He ran the flame up and down the doll and it flickered and danced in the usual manner.

Letting the flame die, Albert rubbed his chin. "Huh."

"Flame isn't the reactant?" Duncan asked.

"Doesn't seem to be." Albert grabbed a jar of spices, sprinkling them across the doll. Nothing happened. "Doesn't seem to be related to common herbs, either."

"So it's not a curse?" Nelson asked.

Albert frowned. "There's one last thing to try, but I hate to think it." He took a small needle from amongst the supplies on his table and pierced a hole on the tip of his finger.

He squeezed and one small drop of blood fell from his hand and down onto the doll.

And it instantly sizzled where the blood touched and the doll began bouncing on the table like a fish flopping out of water.

"Oh, dear." Albert rubbed his chin.

"I take it we don't want blood to be the reactant?" Duncan asked, looking to the two well-educated men before him.

"Seems to be a blood curse," Nelson explained. "Which means that someone had to have been sacrificed in order to seal this curse."

"Yes," Albert agreed. "Someone died. And their death was the reactant." Albert looked soberly up at Duncan. "And those are the hardest curses to undo."

"So, the powerful and angry spirit that is haunting the Reisers' house is tied to this doll through a blood curse?" Duncan asked in order to make sure he was clear on all the specifics they had thus far.

Albert nodded. "The spirit cannot crossover because of the blood tie to this doll."

"And if there are other ghosts in the house? How does that affect things? Or does it?" Duncan asked.

Albert frowned. "I've never seen that type of situation."

So Nelson interjected, "We have. Whenever we've seen multiple spirits, Duncan, one entity is feeding off the others."

Duncan ran his hands through his long bangs. "Jane did say she needed souls."

"Oh, dear," Albert said again.

"What? What could that mean?" Duncan asked the demonologist.

"Well, from what I've read it's like a vacuum cleaner," the professor explained. "A cursed spirit can literally suck other souls into the curse. My guess is any other entities you've encountered are part of the curse now."

"But we don't know what the curse is yet,"

Duncan frowned. "Just the fact that there was a curse, right?"

"You can usually get contextual clues from the things that happen when people associate with this doll," Albert said.

"Well, the women in every household that we know has had the doll have become obsessed with it, to the point of almost choosing it over her family," Nelson told the professor.

"So perhaps the doll has some significance?" Duncan asked.

Albert shook his head. "Or it was chosen completely at random, as an object that just happened to be handy at the time of the curse. The significant thing here is the person who was cursed and why. It must have something to do with abandoning your family."

Duncan looked at Nelson, so Nelson responded with, "Perhaps Esther felt betrayed by Salamander's choosing of Elizabeth? But then Salamander would be the cursed spirit, right?"

"Did you say Esther and Salamander?" Albert asked, eyes widened with surprise at the familiar names.

"Yes, why? What do you know?" Duncan asked quickly, sensing that Albert had light to shed on the narrative.

"Well, it's really just folklore. Urban legend of sorts, if you will," Albert responded and chuckled nervously.

Duncan folded his arms across his chest. "You'd be surprised how often that's important in our line of work. What can you tell us about Esther and Salamander? There wasn't much in the history books."

"Esther is like a boogeyman around these parts." Albert started laughing again before waving fingers in Duncan's face as he said, "She's wandering the streets looking for you. It's ridiculous really."

But Duncan didn't join in the mirth. He felt there was something here. "How did Esther die?"

Albert sobered up a bit to say, "She was lynched. Oh, yes, Esther Robbins was one of the most famous lynchings in this part of the country."

"They caught her freeing slaves to Canada?" Nelson assumed.

"No, that's not what the legend says." Albert had turned serious again. "She was lynched for trying to kill a white man."

"Salamander," Duncan and Nelson both said at the same time.

Duncan pulled out his phone and called Paige. "You can stop researching, Paige. We know what happened to Esther and it wasn't good." He put the phone on speaker and set it on the table. "All right, Albert. Tell us everything you know."

Chapter 12 – The Lynching Legend

"As an academic, I must state this disclaimer before I begin. Nothing I am about to tell you will be found in history books of any repute. It's local legend only." Professor Albert Dupree, the demonologist, looked uncomfortable as he leaned back against the table to retell the tale of Esther Robbins.

Duncan nodded at the professor. "We understand that. You might be surprised how often things related to our cases are based on things people do not like to document."

Albert nodded in response. "The urban legend is that Esther wanders the streets searching for her lost love so she can finish the job of murdering him. But because she's dead and doesn't know it, she often chooses any man she encounters. Of course, she never kills such men, just brings them discord and bad luck,"

Albert continued. "It's a cautionary tale to young people to be careful who you date or Esther will come and get you. That kind of thing. But no one takes it too seriously. It's more like a campfire ghost story people laugh at."

"So could this be why she sucks the women she encounters into her curse? So she can attach herself to their husbands?" Duncan asked.

Albert frowned. "I suppose it could be."

Through the phone, Paige's voice reverberated. "So what happened to the real Esther? Legends are often exaggerated versions of the truth."

"Well, again, history books are lean on the subject. But the tale goes that Esther had tried to murder a white man and was therefore lynched by a white mob and strung up a tree," Albert continued, frowning as he told the awful story.

"Oh, that's horrible," Paige said through the phone.

"Was the white man Salamander Guillame?" Duncan asked.

Albert shook his head. "I can't say for sure. The legend just says she was lynched for her attempted murder and now wanders the streets looking for her man."

"If Esther was lynched, then she had to have been cursed before the lynching," Nelson added.

"No one would have more reason to curse her and have her lynched than Elizabeth Guillame," Paige said.

"So are we thinking Elizabeth either curses Esther or has her cursed, and then accuses her of attempting to murder Salamander? Knowing that as a black woman the angry mob would come for her?" Duncan asked the team, his hands resting on the top of his head, his curly hair going every which way between his fingers.

"It tracks," Nelson responded.

"It makes sense to me. Yes," Paige added through the phone.

"And then as her spirit encounters other ghosts, she sucks them into her curse, also?" Duncan asked.

"The curse vacuum," Nelson nodded.

"Is that a thing?" Paige asked.

"As the theory goes," Duncan confirmed.

"So we need to find the origin of the curse so we can undo it," Paige responded.

"I think that will be your biggest challenge." Professor Dupree rubbed his chin. "Even assuming you can find the origin of the curse upon Esther, undoing a blood curse is tricky, at best."

"How so?" Duncan asked.

Nelson looked at Albert and sensed his trepidation, so he answered on the professor's behalf. "You know how we usually undo curses?"

"Yeah," Duncan answered without hesitation. "Once we know what constituted the curse, we use those components to undo it. Reverse engineer of sorts."

Nelson nodded with his eyes wide.

And then realization hit Duncan. "Oh. We have to use blood."

And Nelson looked over at Albert one more time. "Weeelllll...." He dragged the word out, his discomfort carrying the syllable across the lab and filling the room with a foreboding.

At Nelson's response, Duncan's eyes went as wide as his teammate's. "So someone has to *die* to undo Esther's curse?"

"I'm nervous that that might be the only way to undo this one," Albert answered cryptically.

"There has to be another way." Paige's bubbly voice came through Duncan's phone with an air of optimism that wasn't physically in the room with the men.

"Professor Dupree, why would someone use blood as the curse reactant instead of fire or something more mundane?" Duncan asked.

"Fire certainly aligns with the evils of Hell, but dark forces require more." Albert's eyes darkened as he described the sinister topic. "Blood is the essence of life. The very symbol of our mortality. To take any kind of covenant up a notch requires life source.

Blood. Or death. Or both. It's next level on the evil scale."

"So do the tales of Esther's lynching include blood at all? I mean, if it was death by hanging, perhaps there was no bloodshed." Nelson looked around the room with hope in his eyes, but it was clear that he didn't actually believe his own theory.

Albert shook his head. "Sadly, no that is not the case. She was beaten first. It was a brutal death."

"And then the curse was sealed. That she would be tied to the earth for eternity trying to find Salamander to finish what she started," Duncan frowned.

"Which was?" Paige asked.

"To kill the white man," Albert explained.

"That doesn't align with the real story, though," Paige replied. "She loved Salamander. She absolutely did not want to kill him, whatever happened."

"Even if he married another woman and she was angry?" Duncan asked.

"She was hurt, no doubt. But if she was going

to resort to murder, wouldn't she murder Elizabeth?" A pause where Duncan could imagine Paige shaking her head vehemently. "No, I can't believe she tried to murder Salamander. It just doesn't add up."

"But the cursed spirit of Esther hasn't murdered anyone," Nelson explained, adjusting his black-rimmed glasses. "If she was out to finish any kind of job, she would have done so by now. That part is just the line of truth blurred with the cover-up story. No, I'm certain Elizabeth just made the whole thing up. I highly doubt she needed any proof at all. Just the accusation alone would be ample."

"I suppose you have a point there," Paige said. "The doll makes women morose and the families miserable, but not dead. So the curse is really that she pays her hurt and anger forward with the families she encounters."

"And the souls she sucks into the curse are from people who've died naturally," Duncan added.

"So who exactly was Elizabeth Guillame? And why was she playing with the Dark Arts?" Professor

Dupree added.

"Do you know what I want to know?" Paige asked. "If Esther is the woman tied to the doll, and Jane is one victim that Esther is feeding off of, who is the third ghost? I'm guessing now it's not Salamander because I think the curse would play out very differently if she were tied for eternity to her lost love."

"I agree, Paige," Duncan responded. "So I think our next step is to answer these questions. You get started on researching Elizabeth Guillame, especially any rumors that might have gone around about her. Nelson and I will rejoin Duane and hope he has something in the footage that gives us more clues about the man with the heavy footsteps."

Nelson raised a hand timidly. "And if the only way to undo the curse is with a death? What do we do then?"

A heavy silence filled the room like a thick fog. No one dared voice the fact that this may be the first time when a client, and their haunting, might be unhelpable.

Chapter 13 – The Third Ghost

The room was dark and with his headphones on, Duane could completely submerge himself into his job of reviewing footage. For once, his black hoodie was down, revealing his tattooed bald head. Every time they went to the Reisers' bungalow, they caught more stuff on camera. Some hauntings they were called to they considered themselves lucky to capture any evidence at all.

But this case was an avalanche of paranormal activity.

And he was in the zone. Watching. Documenting. Saving clips. He loved this part of the job.

So when Duncan and Nelson stormed into his hotel room and turned on the light, he reacted violently to the sharp brightness in his eyes.

"We need everything you've got on the third ghost," Duncan announced, flopping his large body on the edge of the bed.

Still shielding his eyes to the bright light, Duane answered, "And you couldn't knock first because...?"

Ignoring Duane's outburst, Nelson added, "The man. The entity with the heavy footsteps. What do you have on that guy?"

"I have plenty." Still rubbing his eyes, he disconnected his headphones from his computer and clicked on a folder where he was keeping the clips of all his evidence. "Click on these."

With Nelson over his shoulder, Duncan took Duane's place at the computer and started clicking, just as Duane had instructed.

The first clip was simply audio. A snippet of the heavy footsteps. Multiple people had heard that by now, so for sure they had a third ghost and he enjoyed stomping around.

The second clip was a video. Indistinct and fast, Duncan and Nelson could barely make out a wisp of something akin to smoke swirling past the camera. If they hadn't known what to look for, they surely would have missed it.

"Do you have anything that would give us a clue as to who this ghost might be? What his story is?" Duncan asked Duane without looking at him. Patience had never been a virtue of Duncan's. He preferred to jump to the good stuff rather than spend any amount of time digging through all the clips Duane had gathered.

"Clip 17," Duane grunted at his team leader.

Without spending any additional time asking or thinking about Duane's suggestion, Duncan clicked on clip 17. Duane might be short on words, but he was trustworthy and a very good investigator. A small part of Duncan had to admit that Duane was better than he was. At least when it came to finding and gathering evidence. No one else could compare to Duane. No one else had the meticulous eye that he had.

The window with clip 17 opened in the foreground and the Reisers' front room near the dining area could be seen. You could hear people talking in the background. Paige's voice was explaining what she had found about Salamander Guillame.

And then a face was in the camera.

And it wasn't Duane's. It was an older man. An older man that none of them had seen or noticed in the room with them. They had heard him plenty enough and knew he was there.

But they would have remembered that face.

He looked to be in his early sixties, weathered skin and salt and pepper hair. The old man tilted his head to one side as he investigated the strange equipment he stared into, never knowing that it was simultaneously capturing his every move. He was solid. Not wispy like in the other clip. Duncan could see the lines on his face and the blue speckles in his hazel eyes.

And then he vanished.

"Whoa! That's a great piece of evidence, Duane. I wish we could show the client. I mean, you really captured a ghost's full face!" Duncan leaned back in his chair. "Does he ever say who he is?"

Duane stared at Duncan for a silent moment. And then he said, "You can see his face. In detail."

"Let's have Paige find a photo of every man who ever lived in this house and we can compare it to the clip," Nelson suggested.

Duncan raised an eyebrow. "Or every man sucked into the curse of the doll. I can't put my finger on it, but he seems familiar somehow." Duncan pulled out his phone and dialed. "Shawna? It's Duncan again from the Paranormal Investigators League. I have what may seem like a strange request." A pause while Shawna responded to this random caller. "Can you send me a picture of your father? Perhaps when he was in his sixties?" Another pause. "And if it isn't too rude of me to ask, how did your father die?"

When the call ended, Duncan stared at his phone, waiting for the satisfying beep that announced his notifications.

"Mr. Holden died of a heart attack at seventy-one," Duncan explained as he waited. "And his daughter, Shawna, is sending me a picture."

"But it could be anyone over multiple generations. What made you think it was Mr. Holden?" Nelson asked.

"Well, it is a bit of guess-n-check for sure," Duncan responded. "But Shawna had told me her mother was obsessed with the doll, so I assume the curse affected her. And if Mr. Holden was the Salamander stand-in for the curse, perhaps this was his fate when he died." Duncan shrugged. "Just a hunch."

Then his phone chimed the notification bell.

As fast as his fingers were able, Duncan opened the image attachments Shawna had sent him. And a handsome man with bright blue eyes stared back at them, hugging a woman Duncan assumed was his wife.

And this man was definitely not the man in the footage.

"Rats," Duncan exclaimed, chewing his lip.

"It was a longshot." Nelson rested a supportive hand on Duncan's large shoulder.

"It was a piss in the wind," Duane groaned.

"Duane, send me this clip, please," Duncan instructed. "Nelson, you and I are going to meet Paige at the library. We've got the ghost's face. We should be able to see which homeowner he is."

"And what then?" Duane asked, still slumped in his chair where he'd been all day watching and editing. "Is he part of the curse?"

"Yes," Nelson nodded. "The doll is associated with the Underground Railroad heroine Paige told us about. Esther Robbins. And her curse sucks other souls into it."

"A curse vacuum," Duncan added.

"I don't buy it," Duane said simply.

"No, it's awful. It was a blood curse," Nelson continued trying to persuade his investigator.

"Exactly my point, Nelson." Duane looked up at Nelson. "The doll represents a dark and evil curse that sucks in other souls for one-hundred and fifty years, but we only have three ghosts?" Duane shook his head. "I've been watching footage for days now. There are no other ghosts. I think your vacuum theory has some holes."

Duncan rubbed his chin as he mulled over Duane's words.

"No chance of other ghosts?" Nelson asked.

Duane shook his head. "We have a lot of evidence. I mean, a lot. And it's very clearly three ghosts. The lady obsessed with the doll, the little girl and the old man. That's it."

"You make a valid point, Duane." Duncan pulled his bangs back with entwined fingers, resting them on top of his head.

"So, no curse vacuum?" Nelson asked.

"No, I mean about the female ghost being obsessed with the doll. What if we have the curse all wrong?" Duncan asked, looking up at Nelson.

And the realization dawned. "So what if the doll isn't the binding agent, you mean? What if the doll is the curse?"

"And the female ghost isn't tied to the doll, she's protecting it." Duncan frowned.

"Then this could be worse than I thought." Nelson pursed his lips.

"What are we thinking, Nelson?" Duncan asked.

"A blood curse for Esther to be tied to the earth for all eternity spreading malaise was bad enough, but a cursed object tied to a death is the granddaddy of curses. I'm thinking we may not be able to get rid of this haunting."

"But what if we don't have to undo the curse?" Duncan asked, standing up with a jolt of energy. "What if we just need to help our clients? We just have to get the cursed object out of here."

"And wrap it in something blessed and store it somewhere safe. Otherwise, we're just shifting the curse to someone new." Nelson folded his arms across his chest.

Duane still sat slumped in his chair. "Not good enough. We have to help the ghosts too. It's what we do." And without further ado, he put his headphones back on, rolled his chair over to the light switch and flipped the room back to total darkness.

Chapter 14 – Elizabeth and the Curse

"Did you figure out who the thumping ghost is?" Paige asked as she bounced over to Duncan and Nelson at the front of the library.

"Sort of," Duncan answered. "We have his face, so now we just have to match it to various owners of the house."

"You make that sound easy. They don't keep photographs of the homeowners next to the deeds in public record." Paige shifted her weight to one leg, staring at her co-investigators as if they had no respect for her role as researcher.

"There's more," Nelson responded instead of acknowledging Paige's accusation. "The curse may not be what ties the ghosts to the doll."

"That's actually really interesting." Paige stared at Nelson.

"Right? Duane mentioned that the lady ghost was obsessed with the doll and that got me thinking," Duncan explained.

"No. I'm saying it's interesting because of what I found on Elizabeth Guillame." Paige put her hands on her hips. "I was going to tell *you* that I thought we might have had it all wrong."

"Tell us what you've got, Paige." Duncan folded his arms across his chest, waiting for the details on this case to finally fall into place.

Paige leaned in with a glee-filled smile. She loved juicy updates like this one. "This lady was as evil as they come. Narcissistic, manipulative, vengeful. She never lured Salamander away from Esther. She blackmailed him!" Paige paused for dramatic effect and Duncan just waved her on. Paige clutched her hands to her heart. "Esther and Salamander were always in love. He never betrayed her after all."

"Of course, that's lovely to hear, Paige." Duncan had that brotherly look he sometimes got with her. "But can you please get back to Elizabeth?"

"Yes, well. Elizabeth was born to a lower-class family, but she was a total social climber. But the way she broke into those circles was by digging up dirt on various political leaders, rich men like Salamander and anyone in positions of power. Let's just say she had some friends in low places that would supply her with information. And then she would use it to bribe the men into welcoming her. Once she set her sights on Salamander, he and Esther didn't stand a chance."

"Why didn't she ever go to prison for her actions?" Nelson asked.

"Because." Paige said it like it was the most obvious thing in the world. "She was sleeping with the judge and blackmailing the mayor! She knew way too much."

"So how do we know she has anything to do with the doll? Or do we?" Duncan asked, rubbing his chin. Clearly Elizabeth wasn't going to be winning any Nobel prizes, but it was a big leap to go from social climber to blood curses.

"Oh, we do." Paige smiled again, locking eye

contact with Duncan as she dug in her oversized bag for a printout. "Allow me to read you this." Paige cleared her throat dramatically and then began reading whatever she had found and printed.

"Elizabeth found dolls to be one of the most frightening objects ever made by man. She often used them to intimidate her victims. Mayor Blackwell had received three such porcelain dolls as 'gifts' from Elizabeth throughout his time as mayor. Each one was accompanied with a cryptic note that reminded the recipient of what she knew. Folded papers with scripted handwriting saying things like 'Remember the summer' and 'Gold never lies.' The belief now is that those notes were reminders of whatever she had blackmailed the mayor with, intimidating him into submission and cooperation."

Paige looked up at Nelson and Duncan with a huge grin.

"Okay. So we have a tie to the creepy doll. But our doll has a curse. Is there anything that ties Elizabeth to the occult?" Duncan asked.

"There's nothing that *doesn't* tie her to the occult. She was willing to sink to some pretty low levels. What would a curse be to someone like this?" Paige asked.

"Maybe there's still a curse vacuum," Nelson announced, drawing looks from Paige and Duncan. "So Elizabeth perhaps didn't curse Esther directly because she didn't need to. Having her lynched was curse enough. But what if it was part of her quest for power? What if Elizabeth cursed the doll to bring someone else down to elevate her own station? Does your article list any other recipients of the porcelain doll gifts from Elizabeth?"

"Oh." Paige ran her finger down the printout searching for the right section in the article she'd printed, stopping suddenly and thumping the paper with her pointer finger. "There! Listen." She grabbed the paper with both hands and read, "If you were a prominent figure in Detroit in the 1860's, chances are you were a recipient of an intimidating doll adorned with a threatening note in Elizabeth's own hand.

Perhaps the most enduring story of woe was Carl Hofstetter, who owned the local newspaper. Shortly after receiving his doll from Elizabeth, his home was destroyed in a horrible fire, where he lost everything. Two years later he was arrested and imprisoned for embezzling from the city. Once Elizabeth sunk her teeth into him, his life went to ruin. He always publicly blamed the doll as the harbinger of his doom."

Paige looked up at Duncan and Nelson as realization dawned across their faces.

"That sounds like a cursed doll, all right." Nelson frowned at the prospect of receiving such a gift from Elizabeth Guillame, even as he delighted in the fact they were getting closer to the truth.

"Is there a picture of Carl Hofstetter? I'd like to compare him to our footage of the thumping ghost." Duncan gestured at the article in Paige's hand.

"Right here. Is this your guy?" Paige pointed at a small sepia-colored photograph in the corner of the article. This man had his hair parted down the middle and slicked straight down. He looked wealthy, with his bold chin held high and his fancy clothes.

Duncan shook his head. "No, but I wonder..." Duncan pulled up the clip Duane had given him and played a small bit for them all to watch again. When he pressed pause, he pointed at Paige's handbag. "Do you still have the photo of Salamander?"

Paige's eyes widened and then she dove right in, digging and burrowing around in search of the original printout. When she pulled back her hand, a slightly wrinkled stack of papers emerged. She turned a few pages in. "This is Salamander."

"I thought he looked familiar!" Duncan shouted, slapping his knee with elation at the discovery. "Our thumping ghost is Salamander!"

"Well, I'll be!" Paige beamed.

"So Salamander Guillame and Jane Brillow are stuck for eternity being fed on by Elizabeth Guillame's ghost, who seems to be protecting her cursed doll?" Nelson bounced his theory off his teammates.

"I think so," Duncan nodded, still overjoyed at his own value-add to the investigation.

"Then I think our next step is to separate Elizabeth from the cursed object. We can't just move the doll or she, Salamander and Jane will just go with it."

"I'm in," Paige beamed. "How do we do it?"

"First, we have to understand what Elizabeth used in the first place to create the curse. Then we can use the same methodology to separate her from it," Nelson explained.

Paige shook her head. "There wasn't anything in the article. I mean, it's implied that she was cursing people, among her other unsavory talents, but it doesn't explicitly say she was a witch or anything."

"Then we have to do what we do in these types of situations." Duncan rubbed his hands together. "We have to ask the ghost of Elizabeth Guillame."

"I don't think she is going to play nice. Her only purpose in her afterlife is protecting that doll," Paige responded, still gripping the printouts in one hand and flailing it all over the place every time she spoke.

"Well, I think I may have an idea." Nelson

adjusted his black-rimmed glasses. "We're going to have to make Elizabeth really mad."

Chapter 15 - A Curse, A Doll and a Ghost

"Duane, can you film everything? We want to try and capture anything we learn in case we need to reference it later." Duncan spoke to his bald investigator as they set up another night of investigating in the Reisers' brick bungalow.

And Duane grunted in response.

"I'll be the one to go under. It was my idea," Nelson offered.

"Fine with me. I hate the Estes Method," Paige responded as she pulled out the noise-cancelling headphones and handed them to Nelson. The plan was to lure Elizabeth out by grabbing and burning the doll, and then one of them would promise to stop torturing the doll if she answered questions. Nelson would be interpreting the answers via the Estes Method, which required the investigator to block out all senses and just focus on what was coming through the spirit box.

Nelson stood with the blindfold in one hand and the headphones in the other. He had no intention of jumping into sensory deprivation a millisecond before he had to.

"Here's the spirit box." Duncan plopped a small radio-looking handheld device into Nelson's hand where he held the blindfold. He then proceeded to put on thin medical gloves so he could torture the doll without actually touching it.

Nelson chose a corner of the room where he could lean his back against the wall. The Reisers still had no furniture since they refused to move in until the ghosts were gone. But if you were going to be deaf and blind and trapped with three ghosts, he didn't want to be standing and wobbling on two feet. He'd seen firsthand what Elizabeth was capable of when she was angry. He plugged the headphones into the spirit box and waited for the signal.

"Paige, let's you and I find the doll and then we

can begin the interrogation," Duncan stated.

"Wait." Duane walked over to Duncan and placed a lighter in the palm of his large hand. "To torture the doll."

Paige looked from Duane to Duncan. "Why do I feel a little guilty when you put it that way?"

"Nelson. We'll shout when we find the doll. That's your cue to go under," Duncan instructed.

Nelson nodded and then added, "What will you shout? We should have a codeword. Just in case you have to shout… for other reasons."

"Fine. The code word is 'lion'." Duncan started to walk down the hall and begin looking for the doll, when Nelson yelled after him.

"Lion? Why lion? Why not something more related to Elizabeth?" Nelson asked.

Duncan kept walking but Paige stopped to explain. "Because we're in Detroit, Nelson. The Detroit Lions?"

Nelson looked at her blankly. "I don't get it."

Duane pointed down the hall. "He never will,

Paige. Go find the doll."

With a nod, Paige continued down the hall behind Duncan. Seeing that he was already in the back room with the built-in shelves, Paige turned immediately left and into the first spare bedroom.

It was late and all the lights were off, but the moonlight streamed in through the uncovered window and lit the room with an unsettling glow. Paige could sense the heaviness of a presence and the feeling of being watched.

But she saw no doll.

"Elizabeth? Is that you?" Paige called into the darkest corners of the room. After a beat with no response, she tried, "Jane? Salamander? Are either of you here with me?"

She felt a cold gush of air rush past her, sending her short hair whipping all around her face. She had originally planned to check the closet but decided to follow her instinct instead. Whoever this ghost was, they were leading her to the doll.

She stepped out of the bedroom and into the

hallway, where she caught a glimpse of Duncan stepping into the primary bedroom situated right across from the back room he'd been in. And she waited for the next clue from the ghost.

A knock on the wall near the front room pulled her attention away from the back of the house.

"Was that you, Paige?" she heard Nelson call.

"No. One of the ghosts is leading me to the doll." Paige walked slowly toward the front of the house, feeling the steadiness of the wall as she walked.

"What if it's tricking you? What if it's Elizabeth leading you away from the doll?" Nelson asked.

Paige shook her head even though she was still in the hallway and out of sight of Nelson. "I don't know how I know. I just know. They're helping me."

Loud footsteps thumped across the front room near the corner where Duane was standing. He panned the camera as the sound walked by. As Paige emerged from the hallway, she pointed questioningly in the direction she thought the steps might be headed. Duane gestured with his chin in the direction of the kitchen.

"Salamander? Where are you taking me?" Paige rounded the corner, still walking slowly and deliberately. She trusted her gut that this was a helpful spirit, but there was still that nagging part of her brain that agreed with Nelson. This could be a trap.

But the second she walked into the kitchen, she shouted, "Duncan! I got it." And she came back into the front room with the old, porcelain doll, clutching it in hands that were covered by her sleeves pulled past her fingers. She didn't want to risk touching it and then becoming obsessed with the doll as the women it often encountered were wont to do.

Duncan came thundering down the hallway, his heavy frame making his steps sound like Salamander's, holding the lighter in his gloved hand. "Perfect. Time to torture the doll."

Paige stepped forward to meet Duncan halfway and as she moved forward, the doll left her hands and flew through the air, landing in the middle of the room. Duncan stepped toward the doll and it slid toward the built-in bookshelf on the other side of the room near Nelson.

"Nelson! Lion. Lion, Nelson!" Paige shouted at her co-investigator.

"Lion?" And then realization dawned. "Yes! Lion." He placed the headphones on his ears and secured the blindfold.

Meanwhile, in a rare show of any type of athleticism, Duncan dove on top of the doll and clutched it like a football after a fumble. Holding it tight to his chest as he sat up, he held the lighter up to the face of the doll as if he were in a hostage situation. He was even breathing hard from the exertion.

"Elizabeth. We need answers or the doll gets it," Duncan called out between heavy breaths.

"Dark," Nelson repeated what was coming through for him.

Paige did a dramatic shiver. "I hate torturing an effigy of a small child."

"It's an evil, cursed doll, Paige. Not a who, a what." Duane stared at her and she could only roll her eyes at him in response.

"Are you a witch, Elizabeth?" Duncan ignored Paige's crisis of conscience and plowed forward with getting the details they needed.

"Not...evil." Nelson translated the cryptic message.

Duncan looked at Paige with skepticism. "Not evil?"

"Sounds like something an evil person would say," Paige frowned.

"Doll," Nelson stated.

"The doll isn't evil?" Paige asked.

"What's the curse, Elizabeth?" Duncan asked.

"Moon," Nelson announced.

"A moon rite, maybe?" Duncan interpreted.

"Revenge." Nelson's head was moving side to side as he concentrated on the words coming through only to him on the spirit box.

"We know. You used the doll to curse your enemies, Elizabeth. We need to know how." And to up the ante, Duncan flicked his thumb and the flame from the lighter burst forth.

"Revenge," Nelson said again. And then, "Victim."

Duncan looked at Paige. "Revenge victim?"

"Maybe one of her victims used the doll to get back at her?" Paige shrugged.

"Yes. Victim.," Nelson answered, his eyes still blindfolded, his ears still covered with the noise-cancelling headphones, completely unaware of the conversation he was having on behalf of the spirit.

"Elizabeth? Was this doll a curse on you?" Duncan decided to ask directly.

"Yes. Victim," Nelson stated again.

"Well, I'll be." Duncan shook his head. "We can help you. You need to tell us how to undo the curse."

"Moonlight. Blood," was Nelson's cryptic answer.

"Sounds like witchcraft," Paige said to Duncan.

From behind them and across the room, Duane offered, "The Celts have a ritual that uses moonlight and blood. Typically a bird is sacrificed. It's a way to bring back balance in the world when you've been wronged."

"As in, revenge?" Duncan asked, dropping his thumb and letting the flame die down.

"Essentially." Duane grunted.

"So, Elizabeth's past actions finally caught up to her." Duncan placed the doll gently on the ground and stood up.

"She angered a witch or warlock." Paige shook her head. "It's all fun and games until someone curses a doll to get even with you."

"Can you lead the ritual that undoes the curse, Duane?" Duncan asked, full confidence in the answer.

But Duane turned his crystal blue eyes under his black hoodie straight to Duncan. "It won't work if she doesn't repent for what she did. It's not a curse, it's balance. She has to tip the scales back."

Duncan bit his lip in thought.

To fill the silence, Paige proposed, "People get clarity when they die. Maybe she already knows what she did was wrong. Okay, so Elizabeth deserved the curse for what she did to people in her time, but people in our time are having their lives affected. The balance is gone. This has gone too far."

"Judge," Nelson blurted.

Paige sighed. "I'm not trying to be judgmental. I'm trying to protect the innocent victims who have come in contact with the doll."

"No, not judging. The *judge*." Duncan crossed over to Nelson. "Is that who cursed Elizabeth?"

"Wife," Nelson stated.

Duncan and Paige exchanged a look, and then they both said in unison, "The judge's wife."

"Elizabeth tangled with the wrong witch," Duane stated from underneath his hood.

Duncan yanked the headphones off Nelson's ears. "Nelson. We got it. A blood and moon ritual performed by a witch as revenge for everything Elizabeth did to the judge."

Nelson yanked off his blindfold, eager to shed the sensory deprivation, and joined his fellow investigators in standing in the empty living room. "A witch?"

"So Elizabeth just needs to repent for everything she did to the judge and we can undo the curse!" Paige did a little hop in place at the prospect of ridding the world of yet another curse.

"Are we sure she'll repent? She seems to be enjoying her afterlife tied to an evil doll, if I may interpret the hauntings associated with it." Nelson rested his hands on his hips.

Duncan scratched his chin. "I'll admit we may have been a tad too optimistic."

As if in response to their conversation, the spirit box in Nelson's hand began to emit a crackle of radio static. First one crackle and pop, then another. As Nelson lifted the device to ensure that he hadn't accidentally done something to make the sound erupt, the static intensified and became constant.

"You had it right the first time." A male voice from within the static echoed throughout the empty room. "Elizabeth is the witch and she's protecting..."

And the box went silent and flew from Nelson's

hands and across the room.

"You mean I did the Estes Method for a bunch of lies?" As Nelson followed the flying spirit box, thumping footsteps began to echo all around the investigators. They could see nothing, but behind the heavy footfalls they began to hear a high-pitched scream. It circled them like a hawk circling its prey, hovering and menacing as it chased the footfalls.

"Guys. You should come check this out." Duane calmly gestured to the camera he was standing behind and using to capture footage.

Nelson picked the spirit box off the floor where Elizabeth, presumably, had sent it flying, and joined Duane behind the camera. "Wow. That's great."

"What is?" Duncan asked as he started toward the camera to see for himself.

And then, with a final screech from the spirit above them, the camera shut off and was knocked over, skidding across the empty floor.

"Come on. Really? This equipment is so expensive!" Duncan dropped his arms in frustration.

Chapter 16 – Breaking the Curse

"I really don't like Elizabeth." Duncan shook his head as the team regrouped back at their hotel near the Reisers' home. They needed to plan how to stop the witch and her curse and decided it was best not to do it in front of the witch herself. The air all around them was thick with tension. They were up against a clock with very nervous clients and a mystery that kept unraveling and changing course at every turn.

"You're such a cheapskate, Duncan. The camera is fine." Duane held it up to show Duncan there was no need for concern.

"Show them the footage, Duane," Nelson said. Then to Paige and Duncan he added, "It's really compelling."

Duncan and Paige squeezed in around Duane, all of them sitting on one not-big-enough couch in the hotel lobby. It was sage green polyester and matched the muted earth tones that adorned the hotel itself. A giant painting of a forest accented the wall behind them.

Duane pressed play and, just like the footage in the clip Duane had shown them earlier in the day, Salamander Guillame was seen clearly in full body form. Their eyes hadn't seen anything, but the camera was able to capture him. He was running and looking over his shoulder.

"That's great. He always comes in so clearly for the camera!" Duncan clapped his hands together once in emphasis.

"That's nothing. Watch this," Duane said.

And half a second later, a woman in white with long, flowing hair and arms outstretched came into view. And she was clearly chasing Salamander. And it wasn't see-through, or a shadow, or misty. She was solid form, looking like anyone else in the room.

Only they hadn't seen a thing with their naked eyes.

"Oh. This curse is doing nothing for her complexion." Paige frowned, commenting on how the beautiful Elizabeth had gone from an attractive woman in life, to a wicked old witch in her afterlife. Her face was pale and gaunt, her bones protruding from her joints, her jaw slack as she screamed and chased her husband.

"So, she isn't sorry for anything she's done. And Salamander is a victim, trying to stop his oppressor. That much is clear." Duncan spoke his thoughts out loud.

"The energy is very strong in that house. We've never captured so many full bodies on video before at any other investigation," Duane added.

"The curse vacuum." Nelson sat back and folded his arms in punctuation.

"Whatcha thinking, Nelson?" Duncan asked.

"Elizabeth is using the energy of other spirits to keep the curse alive. That's why Jane said she needed souls. None of this is anything without energy."

"What were your EMF readings?" Duncan

asked Nelson.

"They were elevated, but I didn't retake them when she was having her tantrum. My guess is the device would have peaked."

"So. I take it we're not thinking a blood-and-moon ritual will break this easily?" Duncan had to stand because his large frame was so big on the couch and he was on the edge. If he had leaned back, he would have fallen.

"Duane. Rewind the footage." Paige sat up straight and pointed at the phone.

Duane did as Paige asked. He gave her a world of attitude, but at the end of the day she was like a sister to him. And no one knew better than he how precious a sister truly was.

"There!" Paige shouted and pointed when he'd gone back far enough. "Do you see it?"

"Elizabeth looks like a witch. It's good footage, Duane." Duncan ran his fingers through his bangs, slightly annoyed to be distracted from the topic of stopping the curse.

"No, not her full body." Paige shook her head and then turned to Duane. "Although this is very good footage, Duane. Probably the best we've ever captured."

Duane grunted and tossed a chin in her direction. She correctly understood that it was a gesture of gratitude.

"What is it we're looking at, Paige?" Duncan asked, his hands still resting on his head.

"Look here." Paige pointed at the witch, frozen in time by the pause button, arms outstretched in an eternal chase of her husband. "Around her neck. I bet that symbol means something."

Nelson and Duncan leaned in to look where Paige was pointing. Around Elizabeth's neck, as clear as the image was of the woman herself, hung a large black necklace in the shape of an upside-down triangle. Behind it were red jewels that made the triangle appear to be on fire.

"I've seen that before." Nelson stood up when the realization hit him.

"What is it? Is it a clue to her coven?" Duncan asked.

"Is it the type of magic she used to perform?" Paige suggested.

"It's even simpler than all that." Nelson grabbed the laptop from Duane's lap and typed in a search query. When he found the article he wanted, he turned the laptop around to show the team. "It's a Wiccan symbol. An alteration of the pentagram. The pentagram denotes earth, air, fire, water and spirit. But when you only use the triangle, you are ruling out certain elements."

"Earth, fire and spirit. And she erased the circle of life that usually surrounds it, instead backing it up with destruction. It's a perversion," Duane stated.

"*She's* a perversion. She used her talents to curse people and ruin their lives," Paige frowned.

"Do you know how to undo it, Duane?" Duncan asked.

"Two things. Take away her power over those three elements. And remove her energy sources."

Duane spoke from beneath his hoodie, no inflection in his tone.

"So, we need to help Jane and Salamander and any other ghosts caught in her vacuum to cross over." Paige bounced in her seat, buoyed by a solution at long last. "That doesn't seem so hard to do."

"Unfortunately, I don't think it will be that easy," Nelson frowned.

"What do you think we're dealing with, Nelson?" Duncan rubbed his chin, as he too bounced around the prospects of what lay ahead.

"We can't undo her power without removing the souls, but we can't remove the souls without undoing her power. They're united as one now," Nelson explained.

"So what do we do?" Paige asked. "How do we save Jane and Salamander?"

"How do we help the Reisers," Duncan clarified. The Reisers were clients. Jane and Salamander were ghosts. Not that he wished any ill will toward ghosts; he just wanted to keep priorities in order.

Paige nodded in agreement that the Reisers were the priority, even though she still felt strongly that Jane and Salamander were victims too. In some ways, being cursed in eternity felt worse than what the Reisers had gone through in the very limited time they had even spent near the house or the doll.

"I think the trick will be one of timing." Nelson shifted forward as he explained, using his hands to demonstrate. "Duane and Paige can focus on the elemental spell to remove the power of Elizabeth's curse, while Duncan and I force the souls to cross over."

"When you say 'force'?" Duncan winced, not sure he loved the sound of Nelson's plan.

"It won't be like a normal crossover, where you lure souls into the light. This time they are tethered to Elizabeth's curse, so they will struggle even if they want to go," Nelson explained.

"Still doesn't seem too awful," Paige said, ever the optimist, a slight lilt to her tone as if she was trying to convince her team and ask them to agree all in one sentence. "We've had to do worse to undo a curse. And no one has to die anymore, right?"

Nelson and Duncan turned directly to Paige.

"Sadly, that's not completely accurate," Nelson frowned.

"She used blood to create the curse. We have to use blood to undo it." Duncan folded his arms, a daunting darkness washing over him and creating new lines on his face. He wasn't completely sure who was going to die, but he remembered the words of Professor Dupree all too well.

"That stupid doll," Duane grunted.

"It all goes back to that stupid doll." Nelson shook his head as he agreed with Duane.

"So if Duane and I are undoing the elemental spell and you two are helping souls cross over, how do we undo the blood curse with the doll? I assume it all has to happen at once?" Paige asked, looking from investigator to investigator.

She wanted simple and clean. Go in, get the back story, resolve the haunting. They did it all the time.

Why was this one any different?

"We might need reinforcements." Nelson craned his neck to look up at Duncan looming over him.

Duncan rubbed his chin. "Fine. But we need to conduct all the rituals in the backyard. I don't want to have to tell Jensen and Mia that we did witchcraft in their house. I know them well enough to know that won't fly."

Nelson nodded. "They won't take too kindly to fresh blood on the floor."

Paige swallowed hard in an attempt to hide her shock. It was ineffective. "Guys. Where exactly do we think we're going to get blood for this curse? We're not evil witches. I don't want to stoop to that level." She was pleading and whining, and she found the sound of her own voice highly annoying. She'd never had to beg the team *not* to do something in regards to addressing a haunting. She'd always just rolled up her sleeves and done whatever needed to be done.

Curse, counter-curse. Simple.

Duncan didn't respond to Paige. He looked at her for a second with sad eyes. It was clear that the weight of what they were facing was a drain on his conscience too.

But it wasn't going to stop him. He told the Reisers he'd help them and, dammit, that's what he was going to do.

And then he turned to Nelson. "You still have Albert's number?" When Nelson nodded in response, Duncan added, "Then let's go get that blasted doll and send Elizabeth back to where she belongs."

Chapter 17 – The Ritual

The house was dark and empty, so it made no sense to Paige that they slowly opened the back door and broke in like criminals.

Duncan kept the lights off and he moved as softly and gently as a six-and-a-half foot man can. He crept into the dark kitchen with the team close behind him. His large frame blocked any view of what lay ahead, so they could only follow him as quietly as they could. The plan was simple: get the doll and get out. They would meet Albert in the backyard and prepare the various rituals needed to end this curse and its related hauntings.

When Duncan froze suddenly, Nelson smashed into his large back. Paige stopped in time, but curiosity got the better of her and she peered around Duncan.

The witch was standing in the doorway.

And this time they could see her without the use of a camera.

"She's not going to make this easy," Nelson muttered.

"We can take her. She's a ghost." Duane shrugged from the back end of the line.

"If any of us get past, head straight for the doll," Paige instructed.

"Ready? Go!" As Duncan shouted the instruction, he launched his full over-sized frame at the witch in white blocking the doorway. And he was only somewhat surprised when it felt more like hitting a wall than running through a ghost. The witch tossed her head back and laughed, her long, scraggly hair billowing out behind her. "Anyone else got any bright ideas?"

"Oh. I do!" Paige raised her hand high in the air like a kid wanting to be called on by a teacher. "Let's use them."

She pointed around Duncan at a glowing room behind the witch, a gathering of souls trapped in an eternal curse brought on by the entity blocking the doorway. Duncan raised an eyebrow and then said, "Yep. That's a good idea."

"Salamander!" Paige called out to the glowing, faceless crowd. She knew he was there, could sense him. But the only response she got was a shove by Elizabeth that sent her skidding backward across the floor. Her salvation was that Duane was still lurking in the back and was able to stop the momentum before she fell or smashed into the back door.

With barely a glance in Duane's direction to show gratitude, Paige continued on her singular focus. "Salamander! We need the doll. Get us the doll!" Paige shouted from the back of the kitchen.

They had no way of knowing if Salamander heard Paige, and if he did, if he was planning to comply. But they could see Elizabeth.

And she was enraged.

She had centuries of building up the energy to sustain her curse. And that was after a lifetime of controlling other people through nefarious means.

Behind her gathered a small army of souls that were linked to hers.

No way were these four trespassers going to stop the good thing she had going.

Her screech was otherworldly. It was so sharp and painful that Paige had to actually cover her ears to prevent the piercing stab from reaching her eardrum. And as Elizabeth began moving, twirling in place like a witch tornado, she pulled a vortex of energy that felt unstoppable. The room was blown about like an island having its own private hurricane.

Duncan leaned over to his team, shouting to be heard over the screeching and the wind of the energy vortex. "We need to figure out how to get around this. Paige, why don't you and I go around front? Nelson, you and Duane can stay here and distract Elizabeth."

"I don't think blocking two doors will be beyond her skills and abilities." Nelson adjusted his glasses—not an easy feat in the witch's storm. "She was fairly powerful when she *wasn't* really angry with us."

"She can't block every form of entry." Paige crossed her arms, suddenly defiant, even though deep down she really didn't enjoy breaking and entering. She despised Elizabeth even more for pushing her.

"Go." Duane tossed his head over his shoulder, indicating the back door. "I got this."

Paige and Duncan barely stopped to process his words before heading out the back door, this time without the pretense of sneaking around quietly. It had been ineffective anyway. Meanwhile, Duane planted his feet shoulders' width apart and opened his arms like he was a wrestler sizing up an opponent. The witch's mini-storm had blown off his hoodie and he faced her, bald head glowing in the moonlight shining through the kitchen window.

"What do you plan on doing?" Nelson asked.

"We just have to keep her distracted," Duane responded, eyes on the spinning, screaming witch in the doorway.

And then he ran at her, full force, arms outstretched as if he planned to pick her up when he got to her.

He didn't make it very far.

His momentum slowed the closer he got to the angry witch, and his footfalls became slow and heavy, even sliding backward every now and again. It was like walking against a powerful wind, up a hill, with pockets of ice on the ground. He couldn't find the footing to get him close enough to Elizabeth.

But they just had to keep her distracted long enough to sneak Duncan and Paige in through the front door.

"Elizabeth!" Duane shouted, his voice small and distant in the storm all around him. "Your spells suck."

The witch kept screaming and spinning, ignoring Duane completely.

"Maybe if we hug the walls, we'll be out of the vortex enough that we can make it past," Nelson shouted in Duane's ear. Duane nodded and they each took an opposite wall, sliding slowly forward toward the kitchen entrance. And for a minute they thought it just might work. The force shoved them back up against the wall, pressing on their chests like a barbell, but they were able to inch forward toward the dining room.

But a noise at the front door caught their attention. Duane could just barely make out that the door was opening and closing rapidly. She was blocking Duncan and Paige's entrance, just as Nelson had predicted. Whether she was able to spread her presence that wide, or her mini-storm was just that powerful, Duane had no idea. Nor did he care. He needed to do something dramatic in order for all his teammates to get through that front door.

And all he could think of was to match the witch and beat her at her own game.

He ran forward, screaming and spinning as hard and fast as he could.

But for his efforts, he just got launched backward like Paige had a few minutes before. Only this time, he wasn't there to protect himself and he smashed hard into the cabinets against the back wall.

"Ow." Duane rubbed his lower back at the

place of impact.

Nelson just frowned, his usually perfectly-styled hair blowing uncharacteristically out of place. He was too much of a gentleman to tell Duane what a dumb idea that had been, but they both knew he was thinking it.

Out on the front porch, Paige and Duncan were still wrestling with the front door, oblivious to Duane's and Nelson's feeble attempts to help them get inside. But their efforts weren't achieving much more than Duane's.

Duncan was still pushing on the front door as hard as he could when Paige came up with a new idea. "The window in the back bedroom!"

She took off running before Duncan could even acknowledge her idea. But he caught up quickly because he knew he was getting nowhere with the front door and he had long legs so every step was two or three of Paige's. They ran around the side of the house where it felt like a lifetime ago that Duncan had learned about Jill's death from the Reisers' neighbor,

Mr. Elliot Gray.

Paige stopped suddenly at the face in the window before her.

She was shocked and surprised, but it only caused her to falter for a second. She *had* asked him to help her. And he did.

Salamander stood in the window, a shadowy face but clear enough that she knew exactly who it was. He *had* been appearing quite clearly on their footage throughout the investigation.

"Salamander has the doll." Paige pointed at the ghost in the window.

"How do you know?" Duncan asked as he pushed the window up to open it.

Paige shook her head at the back of Duncan's head, eyes locked on the ghostly eyes before her. "I just do."

And then the ghost vanished. But the doll appeared on the windowsill, silently and carefully.

With very little regard for the curse it contained, Duncan grabbed it barehanded and held it up in the moonlight. "This thing certainly has seen some better days, huh?"

"Let's go." Paige tugged on his arm and they ran to the backyard, as far from the house as they could, lest the witch find some way to suck the doll right out of Duncan's large hands.

"Oh, my word!" Albert Dupree rounded the corner of the house from the opposite side of where Duncan and Paige had just been with Salamander's ghost. He repeatedly looked over his shoulder at the flashing and slamming happening in the kitchen thanks to Elizabeth's anger. "What is going on?"

"Nelson! Duane!" Duncan called out and the two investigators came running out the back door, slamming it behind them.

"It's Elizabeth," Paige explained to Professor Dupree. "She didn't want us to get the doll."

Albert Dupree stared in wonder at the lights flashing on and off and the swirl of white spinning in the kitchen. He'd never seen the like.

"You got in," Duane beamed, naturally

assuming his physical sacrifice had been the distraction he'd wanted it to be.

"Salamander gave it to us in the back window," Duncan explained, pointing at the side of the house. "Now, let's get moving. I doubt we have much time before she realizes we have the doll."

Without dwelling on the situation, Duane marched forward to execute the plan like a good soldier. He grabbed the black duffel bag from where he'd dropped it earlier in the evening under a bush. He had prepped the spells ahead of time, so he handed one bottle to Paige and kept the other for himself.

"You'll need blood too." Albert lifted a small vial from his pocket and held it up for the investigators to see.

"I don't even want to know. Just don't tell me." Paige shuddered visibly.

"Relax. It's just one of the lab rats," Albert explained anyway.

"Ugh. I said I didn't want to know! Why would I want an innocent animal sacrificed for any reason?"

Paige yelled at the professor.

"Paige!" Duncan glared at her. "You can write a letter to PETA later. Right now we need to focus."

"*Golau lleuad*," Duane chanted, swaying back and forth like he was in a trance.

"He started, Paige. Join him," Duncan instructed. As she grabbed Duane's hand and began chanting with him, Duncan turned to the Professor. "Start the counter-curse for the blood spell."

Professor Dupree nodded and then knelt next to the vial of blood and the creepy doll placed before him on the grass.

There was a streetlight in the distance, but their only light of any significance was the moon. It gave everything a soft glow, like the very Earth knew a curse was being broken tonight.

"We have to hurry and help those souls, Nelson." Duncan grabbed Nelson by the arm and yanked, although he didn't have to. Nelson was a willing participant and he understood the urgency. They ran to the back door, but before they could even climb the steps, the door burst open and a gust of Elizabeth's ghostly hurricane blew them back.

"Don't stop for anything!" Duncan shouted over his shoulder at Paige, Duane and Albert.

In response, Paige and Duane chanted louder, "*Golau lleuad.*"

Professor Dupree nodded and continued his spell, which looked like he was pouring blood on the doll, but Duncan didn't want to stop and ask questions.

"I don't think we can get in there," Nelson told Duncan. "We have to talk to them from here. They know what to do."

"Jane! Salamander!" Duncan called into the house and then wished he knew the names of the other ghosts feeding Elizabeth's curse. "It's time. You have to cross over. Now!"

The howling wind from inside the kitchen was his only response. The back door flopped open, then closed, then opened again with a bang. The lights inside the house continued to flicker.

Duncan turned to Nelson. "I have to at least try

one more time."

And without waiting for Nelson to talk him out of it, Duncan ran shoulder-first into the hurricane.

He'd never been very athletic. If anything, he was probably a bit on the lazier side. He was well aware of this and always had been. Honestly, he had never even been that bummed about it.

Until now.

Elizabeth's swirl of energy and air shoved him back into the night like she was flicking an ant off the counter. He landed with a heavy thud.

"She's not going to let you...," Nelson began, but Duncan held up a hand. He knew it. He didn't need to hear it. Nelson was right.

"I can help you." A small child's voice floated into their ears.

From the darkness of the backyard, Paige called out, "It's Jill, Duncan. She's outside the vortex!"

Duncan looked up and saw that Paige was right. She was scarcely more than a shadow with a soft, green glow, but the shape of a little girl was unmistakable. And she stood on the steps leading up to the back porch.

"How did you…?" Nelson started to ask, but then realized he wasn't even sure what he was asking.

"I've never been under her control. She's wanted me for as long as I can remember, but I'm free." Jill's soft voice played like a violin, haunting in its ghostly innocence. "And I can help you with the souls."

"I'm almost done undoing the curse," Albert yelled from the darkness. In the shadows, Duncan could see him covered in blood. He looked ghastly.

"Don't stop. If you get to the end, start over," Duncan shouted back. "Nelson and I are going in." With a nod to Jane, Duncan and Nelson stepped forward onto the back porch, a renewed sense of purpose and determination provided by a little girl who died of polio decades before this moment in time. "Lead the way, Jane."

Jane's little shadow turned around silently and the back door flung wide open. They never saw her touch it, but this time the back door stayed open without banging shut. And then Jane lifted her arms wide and the wind in the kitchen seemed to respond as if she were the master and not Elizabeth.

Nelson couldn't help it. He pulled his EMF detector from his pocket and measured the electromagnetic energy coming from Jane. As he'd suspected, his device was pegged.

The energy in this haunting was off the charts.

Duncan braced himself for impact just in case he was flown backwards again. As a big man, he wasn't used to being tossed about. And it hurt. He was sore in places where he wasn't used to being sore. But they were on a clock, and he had to get at least some of those souls to cross over or Elizabeth would continue to be able to use their energy to keep her curse strong, fighting against everything Albert, Paige and Duane were trying to accomplish in the moonlight out back.

So, shoulder-first, he pushed into the kitchen right behind Jane. And this time he was able to get in. However Jane was controlling Elizabeth's tirade, it was working.

Duncan didn't have time to dwell on the how. He had to jump right in. "Hear me, souls of the departed." There was a glow in the Reisers' dining room that equated to all the souls huddled in a corner. In front of them, Salamander stood. If it was possible for a ghost, he looked tired.

"It's time, Salamander." Duncan held an arm out, Nelson right behind him. They both stood barely an inch from where Elizabeth was still screaming and spinning. Kitchen lights were still strobing in the background. She had created a madhouse.

And Salamander didn't want to be here anymore. His ghost turned his head in the direction of the witch who had once been his wife.

"Her power is growing weaker," Duncan said, hoping. "This is your chance."

Nelson held up his EMF detector. The bright lights flashed in the dark room. "It's true. Her hold on you is weakening, Salamander. Go now!"

With a final look at Jill, Salamander disappeared from view. Without a psychic here,

Duncan and Nelson could only assume and hope that it meant he was gone for good.

"It's time. All of you. I'm sorry I don't know all your names," Duncan frowned. He *was* truly sorry about that. They hadn't known she had had so many in her curse until just this evening. Their investigation had only been able to uncover the three, two who were independent—Jane and Elizabeth—and one who must've just been very motivated to resist Elizabeth's power.

Looking at all the glowing souls there in the corner of the dining room, he couldn't be sure, but it didn't look like any of them had left. "Go into the light. It's your time."

And then a small voice from the kitchen. Jill.

"She can't hold you anymore."

And just as she had done with Elizabeth's tirade, Jill controlled the room. One by one, the glowing orbs of spirits trapped on earth began to flicker, dim, and disappear.

"The EMF readings are dropping," Nelson

announced, watching the small device in his hands carefully.

"Nooooooo!" The screech from the kitchen was so shrill that Duncan actually winced at the sound . Elizabeth was furious that her curse was vanishing. The source of her power was disappearing.

And her vortex was slowing down—the wind was beginning to feel more like a fall breeze and less like a hurricane.

Elizabeth flew at Duncan with her arms outstretched and all Duncan could do was brace for the impact, prepare to be thrown across the room.

But instead, she just kept going, through Duncan's body. His long, wavy bangs flew up from the force, but nothing else. Duncan clapped his hands together in relief and joy.

Elizabeth's power on this earth was finally waning.

"Noooooooo...," she howled again. Turning to Duncan, her face contorted with rage, her arms outstretched and her long bony fingers aiming for

Duncan's face. No words were needed. She was clearly expressing her hatred for Duncan.

He braced himself again, prepared for any eventuality. Yes, he knew her curse was weakening, but he had no idea if she had other ways to muster the energy needed to give him one more smack or scratch. He wasn't looking forward to more violence at the hands of this powerful, scorned witch.

But instead, she vanished.

Silence echoed through the house so vividly it actually made their ears ring.

"Can it be?" Nelson asked.

"Is it over?" Duncan asked Nelson, but then turned to Jill.

"She always wanted me." The little girl's ghost was barely more than a shadow, her voice as delicate as a whisper in the wind. "Because I died young, my energy force is stronger than the others. But that's also why she couldn't control me."

"Is she still haunting this home?" Duncan asked, the only question he ultimately cared about. He knew the other ghosts had crossed over, but he needed Elizabeth gone or she could just start everything all over again.

"The doll. It's always been about the doll," Jill's ghost explained. "Without it, she's nothing."

"But we removed the curse…," Duncan started, but then he noticed Jill's shadow had vanished. He looked all around himself, skeptical that she would just leave so abruptly. "Is Jill gone now, too?"

"I think so, Duncan." Nelson put the EMF detector in the pocket of his khakis and started walking toward the kitchen. "EMF spikes are completely gone, so we need to take care of that doll. Just like Jill said."

The scene Nelson and Duncan walked into in the backyard was shady, at best. Professor Dupree had blood on his hands and clothes, and the doll looked like a villain from a horror movie. Paige and Duane were still chanting next to the light of candles in the moonlight.

"Are we done?" Professor Dupree looked

hopeful, despite his bloodbath.

"Smash the doll," Duncan instructed from the back porch.

"What?"

"Smash it. Destroy it. The doll is the vessel. We need it gone," Nelson added. But Professor Dupree still stared up at Duncan and Nelson dumbfounded.

"I got this." Duane walked over to the bloody doll, yanking it none too gently out of the professor's hands, and threw it full force against the back wall.

Nelson frowned. "I think you get far too much joy out of smashing things, Duane."

Without a smile or the slightest hint of the supposed joy, Duane responded, "I do." And then he blew out all the candles and began cleaning up.

Professor Dupree seemed fixated on the shattered doll littering the lawn. "I'm going to keep a piece, if you don't mind. For my collection of cursed objects." He didn't wait for Duncan to authorize it before he bent over and picked up a small piece of the porcelain face.

Duncan shrugged. "Be my guest." Duncan had kept tokens from cases before, but it wasn't really a driving force for him. But he understood that some people needed a tangible piece of their story for future renditions of show-and-tell. He trusted that a professor of demonology would properly care for the remnant of a cursed vessel.

And all of them were completely oblivious to the audience watching everything unfold from across the yard.

Mr. Elliott Gray, the Reisers' neighbor who knew so much about Jane Brillow, leaned over the fence. "So what exactly is going on back here?"

Chapter 18 – The Aftermath

As if the whole world knew the curse was lifted, the sun was shining the next morning and birds provided the cheerful soundtrack. The air was crisp, but not as cold as it should have been for early spring in Detroit. The brick bungalow even had a happy aura about it, sitting there shining in the sun.

And the Reisers stood on the porch, a mixture of hope and fear in their eyes.

"The haunting is over." Duncan spoke in vague details because he was afraid that this may be the first time when knowing too much about the full extent of everything supernatural in your home would backfire. It might cause the Reisers distress rather than some much-needed peace.

"Oh, thank God!" Mia exhaled with gusto, her shoulders physically slumping forward with the release of the tension she'd been clinging to for weeks.

"Yeah. You should be able to move in and sleep soundly." Duncan smiled, opening the door for the couple both to show them it was safe, but also to encourage them to see for themselves.

They took no steps forward.

"What about the doll?" Jensen asked through tight lips.

"Disposed of," Duncan answered cryptically. He stepped inside, hoping that the young couple would follow suit.

"Should we go inside?" Mia asked her husband from the front porch. It was clear she wanted to but was scared. And she certainly wasn't going to without her husband by her side. This couple was one of the most traumatized by their ghosts Duncan had ever seen.

Jensen shrugged. "I guess we have to. We can't live on the porch. And we can't stay in your parents' basement another night."

He took a heavy, hesitant step forward across

the threshold.

"We did a cleansing ceremony on your behalf already, but the EMF readings were already gone the minute that the haunting was over," Duncan explained. "Can you feel the difference?"

Often people could. There was a heaviness when spirits were around watching you. And when they were gone, people often described feeling lighter, less suffocating.

"Yeah. I guess I can." Jensen let the tiniest smile creep across his face.

This was enough for Mia to step inside, holding tight to her husband's side.

"I would burn some sage every now and again, but you shouldn't experience any more disturbances." Duncan clapped his hands together and donned the brightest smile he could paint on his face.

"I never want to see a porcelain doll again as long as I live." Mia shook her head. "Even a sweet-faced, cleaned-up doll. I'll scream."

Duncan nodded in response. "Understandable.

People are often afraid of dolls even without the experience you had with a cursed one."

Jensen raised an eyebrow. "Did you say cursed?"

Realizing he might have let too much slip, Duncan responded too quickly. "It's a long story, but we took care of it. Everything's gone now."

"How do you undo a curse?" Mia asked. But then she quickly waved a hand at Duncan. She was too short to be anywhere near his face, but that's where she would have shaken her hand if she could have. "Never mind. I really don't want to know."

Duncan understood. He didn't want to go into details either. This just wasn't that type of couple. These people enjoyed their ignorant bliss of the paranormal, and he wanted to provide them peace and comfort. It's all he ever wanted for anyone. "The important thing is you can move in. Your haunting is over."

Deep in his soul he wasn't exactly confident that Elizabeth Guillame had crossed over. But he did know that it would take her decades to again amass the kind of power she had recently enjoyed. And she certainly had no control over anyone without her cursed doll, so it felt safe to cajole the Reisers.

"We can't thank you enough." With a nervous laugh, Jensen Reiser extended his hand to Duncan. "We were debating selling the house before we'd even moved in."

Duncan was still shaking Jensen's hand when Mia wrapped her arms around Duncan's large waist. "You don't know how awful it was. We had spent everything we'd ever had on this place."

Duncan patted Mia's back awkwardly. Getting hugged by a client wasn't unusual, but it always felt a little much for him to hug back too warmly. He was a professional, after all.

"I do know how awful it was." Duncan rubbed his back where it still smarted from all the times Elizabeth had tossed him around. "And I'm happy we could give you your house back. It's why we do what we do. You shouldn't have to sell when there is something that can be done to save your dream home."

With another round of 'thank-you's, Duncan let himself out the front door, stepping into the Detroit sunshine. He hoped the Reisers were enjoying their home anew, and that made him smile to himself as he left their brick bungalow, bounding down the front steps.

"You aren't going to tell them, are ya?" Elliot from next door was watering his bushes out front. "About the witchy séance you were doing in their backyard?"

Duncan shook his head as he walked over to the astute neighbor. "Nah. Usually I err on the side of truth." He spared a glance back at the previously haunted bungalow. "But this time I think it's better for the client if they don't know. I think ignorance might be bliss this time around."

"How can you be sure you didn't open a doorway? Instead of sending the ghost away, you called a bunch more in?" Elliot squinted up at the large investigator.

"Oh, no. That's a very different ceremony."

Elliot looked skeptically up at Duncan but didn't respond.

"Can we hit the road now, Duncan?" Duane yelled from the P.I.L. van parked in the street. "I'd like to get home before Paige gets another case and we have to change course."

Paige put on an over-dramatic look of shock. "Who, me? I never take us off course unless it's a true emergency."

"Which is every case," Duane responded.

"You do have a soft spot for people being haunted," Nelson added. "It's not a bad thing."

"I am shocked and appalled." But Paige seemed neither shocked nor appalled as she climbed into Duncan's beat-up old Chevy with a huge grin on her face. Duncan climbed behind the wheel right after her. "Can you believe how they turned on me? After everything I do for this team."

Duncan had to turn the key a few times and prime the gas before the engine turned over. "Paige.

They would both take a bullet for you."

And Duncan pulled out and began the long drive back to California, only sparing one final glance at their latest triumph. He smiled to himself with the tiniest glee over ending an undoable curse and stopping a powerful, centuries-old witch.

And helping one very scared couple finally move into their dream home.

Chapter 19 – Salamander's Story

It was my parents' wealth.

I suppose I enjoyed the fruits of their labor, but in hindsight it really ended up being more of a burden on my life than a gift.

It made me a target.

My forefathers, the Guillame family, had started out as simple immigrants, just trying to make their way in the new land. They'd landed in the French territory near the Gulf, and slowly worked their way up the Mississippi River until they found the region that would change the trajectory of all our lives.

By the time I was born, they had amassed tremendous wealth in the Michigan territory up near Canada and had gobbled up much of the land. My only purpose in life up until the Fugitive Slave Act of 1850 was to toil the land and keep it producing. I had yet to find a wife and yet to produce an heir to the Guillame fortune.

And then I met her.

Esther first approached me because my land was so close to the border. She knew she could hide escaping slaves on my property while they waited for the boat to carry them out of the United States and on to freedom in Canada. Even if the bounty hunters were able to narrow down the escaped slaves' location to my property, I owned so much it would take them days to scour it all.

I didn't care for slavery. I thought it was a very selfish way to make money. My family had done it through hard work and determination. Slave owners had done it on the backs of other people.

But that isn't why I said yes.

I said yes because suddenly my plot of land and all my wealth meant nothing next to something so important. This felt bigger than me. It felt like God had helped my family in the past so that I could, in this moment, pay it forward and help these former slaves escape their tyranny.

That...and Esther was beautiful.

She had stolen my heart from the first moment I had seen her face.

Esther had been on a plantation in Georgia but had escaped with her brother three years prior on the Underground Railroad. She had even made it all the way across the river to Canada. But she knew they could save so many more if I agreed to help.

I believe it was love at first sight because after we met, we were inseparable. Esther lived on my property, helping me work the land by day and then at my side helping runaway slaves escape the bounty hunters by night.

A mere six months later I asked Esther to be my wife.

She turned me down flat. Not because she didn't love me, but because she was worried about our children, if we ever had any. She knew their lives would be horrible. It was hard enough being colored, she told me. But being mixed is even harder.

But I was selfish and wanted Esther no matter

the cost. No one had stolen my heart like Esther had. Beautiful, brave, strong Esther. My heart pines for her still.

My stupid and, dare I say, arrogant heart never imagined a world where I didn't work side by side with Esther. But then one morning, I awoke to find her gone.

At first, I thought nothing of it. A woman as strong and independent as Esther could easily have headed into town or have been meeting with her associates on the Underground Railroad.

I did my work as I always did and waited for her return.

Only that night when Seymour brought around six more negroes searching freedom, Esther wasn't with them. She always accompanied the slaves we freed. She was their lifeline. She was their guide. I asked Seymour about her and he simply shook his head. No one had seen her, he told me.

I never saw my beloved Esther again. I told myself that she decided to live her remaining years peacefully in Canada, her heart loving me so completely that she knew she had to set me free.

But those words I told myself were little comfort. I was so heartbroken I couldn't even imagine myself being with any other woman. I continued smuggling slaves through my property, but I was a ghost of the man I once was. I went through the motions out of obligation. Mostly, I went through the motions in the foolish notion that Esther would return and long to have me back because of all the good I had done. But I had none of the buoyancy in helping these slaves that I had had when Esther was with me.

Until Elizabeth.

I knew her by reputation. I knew people either loved her or hated her. But she was aggressive and determined, and I loved those qualities in a woman. I thought how great it would be to have her at my side helping slaves escape to freedom. And, of course, she loved my money. Once she set her sights on me, I was done for. I had no concept of how done for I truly was.

Of course, in my eyes she was beautiful and courageous. I could almost forget about my beloved

Esther. Almost. It was a hold Elizabeth had over me. I was transfixed by her and consumed by the very thought of her.

And this was, of course, because she had cursed me. I was, quite literally, under her spell.

None of my dreams of Elizabeth ever came true. She didn't care about the Underground Railroad. She didn't want to help anyone other than herself. I was forced to carry on Esther's work in the secrecy of the midnight hour, keeping my life's work and purpose from the one person I was legally bound to.

Meanwhile, Elizabeth lived a double life of her own. I knew she had political ties and ambitions, using my money to sway certain laws to go her way. I just had no idea that she was using all of this to amass her own powers. Well, perhaps I had an idea that something was amiss with her, but I chose to bury my head in the sand. I chose to look away because a part of me just couldn't care. She was my wife and I was legally bound to protect her and provide for her.

Sometimes I look back and wonder if I had really

dug into her late-night musings, would I have stopped her? I'd like to think I would have, but I was weak. In life, I was nothing other than an immature man with nothing to do for most of his days. I had been childish and selfish. Even helping slaves escape—the one good thing I ever accomplished with all the blessings I'd been given—was done mostly to win the heart of my beloved Esther.

So I suppose, ultimately, I deserved to be with someone like Elizabeth. The Guillame family tree would end with two of the most selfish human beings ever to walk the earth. Me, using my money every day to try and once again win the heart of my one true love. And Elizabeth, using my money every day to try and win the hearts and souls of every man in Detroit.

Elizabeth was the more successful of the two of us.

She was strong and beautiful, that much was true. She was cunning and aggressive, also true. And she had a dogged determination to control everyone and everything she came into contact with. You almost have to admire and respect her for that. Had she simply used my money and left me out of her thirst for power, I might have respected her for all eternity.

But, unbeknownst to me, I was one of her earliest victims.

She'd slip her potions into my tea in the morning or my dinner at night—or perhaps both. I could resist her charms and spells no more than someone who'd been hypnotized. I was a sleepwalker in life, and then a steppingstone for her in death.

While Elizabeth was growing in her power over me and others in town, tensions in Detroit were mounting over racial relations. There were many like me who valued the work of the Underground Railroad, who abhorred the atrocities of slavery. But there were many who thought we were simply lawbreakers, helping people who didn't deserve to be helped. Those people slowly became more brazen, attacking negroes in the streets, hunting them down at night, trying to stop the work being done to get them into Canada.

And that's where my story on earth would end.

In March of 1863, the racial tensions would come to a head. Despite Detroit being in free territory, there were many whites who resented the successful and thriving negro community, my wife included. I felt obliged to defend the negroes, knowing many of them personally, having helped them relocate here via the Underground Railroad.

Elizabeth felt that the South needed to win the war for independence so they could get all their slaves back. I thought she was being vindictive. Negroes were good for the local economy and I told her so. They had shops and services and were living good lives here in Detroit.

When I started reading Elizabeth's rhetoric in the paper and hearing it from our city's leaders, I found it odd that they sounded so much like her. Of course, that was for good reason. The white community in Detroit that March was getting angrier and angrier, and that anger turned into a volcano that could only erupt in a very destructive way.

As all major events do, this one began with a

simple act. A white man began beating a black man in front of the courthouse. Perhaps I should have walked on by, but when I realized it was my friend Seymour, my instincts to protect him kicked in.

I was not a fighter. I was not a strong man or a brave man. Or really even an honorable man. I was just a man who happened to be born into a life of privilege. So it should be little wonder that I died that day in the streets of Detroit, defending someone I had come to care for.

My final thought before the light left my eyes forever was an earnest hope and desire that Esther was nowhere near Detroit.

To my horror, I would soon discover how accurate my wish was.

You would think that in death, I would at last be free. Free to spend eternity making amends for my wrongdoings, celebrating my minor triumphs.

But no. Elizabeth took that from me too.

When I transitioned to the spirit realm, the first face I saw was the most beautiful one I had ever known in life or in death: Esther's.

Esther would tell me that Elizabeth had killed her and used her blood in some sort of moon ritual. It was Esther's blood, the blood of the only woman I had truly ever loved, that had given Elizabeth her source of power. Power over me, power over judges and councilmen, power over the city of Detroit.

She sealed it with an unprepossessing porcelain doll and cursed us all to a life and death of pure misery.

Elizabeth turned that cherubic symbol of innocence into her own personal weapon of evil.

As I wandered the streets of Detroit in my afterlife, I grew weary, telling myself that Elizabeth would not live forever and then when she died, Esther and I could be free.

But I was wrong again. My underestimation of Elizabeth and her evil seemed to be another one of my many faults.

In death, she only became more powerful, able to bend both the living and the dead to her whims. The more who died, the more powerful Elizabeth seemed to become. I was distraught in the thought that I would always be subject to Elizabeth's evil.

But then a century later, a little girl named Jane lay dying in her bed. I prayed each night that Jane would recover from her illness, but it wasn't meant to be. She succumbed to the disease that was ravaging her little body and I mourned her life cut short. But Elizabeth cackled with wicked glee. She saw the young girl as a vibrant source of energy—a battery to rejuvenate her supernatural powers.

Only, yet again, it wasn't meant to be.

All the other spirits Elizabeth had gathered over the years, myself included, were cattle. Sheep to her shepherd. But not Jane.

Because of her youth and innocence, Jane was strong and powerful. And filled with benevolence. It turned out that all the reasons Elizabeth wanted her were all the reasons she couldn't control her. Even using the doll, the source of Elizabeth's power.

And once the curse she'd entangled with the doll became disentangled, everything Elizabeth had amassed began to unravel with it.

And now it's my chance to cackle with glee. Vindictive? Perhaps. But I never claimed to be a person of high moral standards. I was just a man who happened to be born into wealth. So much of my life happened to *me instead of because* of *me.*

So my first taste of true freedom came a century and a half after my death. And entering eternity with Esther by my side, I can't help but feel a little smug at the justice. For all of Elizabeth's scheming and conniving to put herself on top, she has landed firmly on the bottom.

And I am the true winner.

Milton Keynes UK
Ingram Content Group UK Ltd.
UKHW030911141024
449705UK00013B/587